Trixie Belden #7

The Mysterious Code

by Kathryn Kenny

illustrated by Paul Frame

cover illustration by Michael Koelsch

Random House New York

Copyright © 1961, renewed 1989 by Random House, Inc. Cover art copyright © 2004 by Michael Koelsch. All rights reserved under International and Pan-American Copyright Conventions. Published in the United States by Random House Children's Books, a division of Random House, Inc., New York, and simultaneously in Canada by Random House of Canada Limited, Toronto. Originally published by Golden Books, an imprint of Random House Children's Books, a division of Random House, Inc., New York, in 1961.

www.randomhouse.com/kids

Library of Congress Cataloging-in-Publication Data
Kenny, Kathryn.
[Trixie Belden and the mysterious code]
The mysterious code / by Kathryn Kenny ; illustrated by Paul Frame. — 1st Random House ed.
    p.   cm. — (Trixie Belden ; #7)
Previously published under the title: Trixie Belden and the mysterious code.
SUMMARY: While preparing for a fund-raiser antique show, Trixie and the other members of the Bob-Whites discover a secret code in the pages of an old magazine in the attic.
ISBN 0-375-82978-4 (trade) — ISBN 0-375-92978-9 (lib. bdg.)
[1. Clubs—Fiction. 2. Ciphers—Fiction. 3. Mystery and detective stories.]
I. Frame, Paul, 1913– ill. II. Title. III. Series.

PZ7.K396Mr 2004 [Fic]—dc22 2003024894

Printed in the United States of America 10 9 8 7 6 5 4

First Random House Edition
RANDOM HOUSE and colophon are registered trademarks of Random House, Inc.

CONTENTS

Chapter 1
No More Bob-Whites?

Trixie Belden rushed into the Sleepyside Junior-Senior High cafeteria. She pushed back her short sandy curls, threw her notebook on the table, and sank into a seat between her two best friends, Honey Wheeler and Diana Lynch.

"What kept you so long?" Honey asked. "We're starved."

"Something terrible!" Trixie gasped when she could get her breath.

"Come on, Trixie, tell us," her brother Mart said. "Don't be so dramatic!"

"I'm not—being—dramatic. Something awful is going to happen to the Bob-Whites of the Glen. Mart, please get Jim and Brian from the kitchen. I want the club members together right now so I can tell all of you."

"Heck, Trixie, they can't leave their jobs at lunch time."

"It's an emergency," Trixie insisted.

"All right," Mart said resignedly, "I'm on my way."

5

Mart, only eleven months older than his thirteen-year-old sister, did not always respond so quickly. Today, though, the tears in Trixie's blue eyes convinced him that she was in earnest.

"Can't you give us a hint?" Diana asked. "You sound as though we were all going to be stricken with some awful plague."

"It's almost worse than that," Trixie sobbed. "Oh, there they are."

"What is it?" Honey's brother, Jim, asked. "Trixie, you're crying. You never, never cry."

"I'm not really," Trixie said and dried her eyes. "It's just this: This morning Mr. Stratton, the principal, stopped me in the corridor and—"

"You're failing in math again," Mart said. "Gleeps, if *that's* all it is—"

"He asked me about the jacket I'm wearing," Trixie went on, scorning Mart's interruption. "I happen to be the only one wearing our B.W.G. jacket today. He wanted to know what is cross-stitched on the back of it."

"Did you tell him it's a secret?" Diana asked indignantly.

"The name isn't, Diana. I told him it stands for our club, the Bob-Whites of the Glen."

"Then what did he ask?" Mart had little sympathy for faculty interference of any kind.

"What the purpose behind the club is," Trixie said.

"Well, that *is* a secret," Honey said.

"I don't believe it is, Sis," Jim said. "In fact we don't have a secret club at all. It belongs just to us, certainly, but it isn't secret."

"Calm down and go on, Trixie." Mart was impatient. "You make such a big deal out of everything."

"I'm not doing it this time, and you'll see. I told Mr. Stratton we were organized just like brothers and sisters, the six of us, to help one another."

"I'll bet that set him back on his feet," said Mart.

"Oh, Mart, listen," Honey insisted. "Go on, Trixie, there must be more."

"Yes, there is, and it's the worst part. I'll die dead if anything happens to the B.W.G.'s."

"It won't," Jim said confidently.

"Mr. Stratton threatened it might," Trixie insisted. "After I told him the purpose of the club he said, 'I don't think that purpose is enough to justify such an organization in the eyes of the members of the school board.' Is that awful enough for you, Mart?"

"Gleeps, yes," Mart said. "Out of a clear sky, too."

"Hardly." They all looked at Trixie's brother, Brian.

7

He was the oldest club member, sixteen, and serious-minded. They paid attention to what he had to say.

"You know the whole school's been talking about the vandalism that's been going on," he said. "Maybe that is what has stirred up the board. You know, worry about gangs forming in Sleepyside."

Trixie jumped to her feet and snapped her fingers. "You're right, Brian," she said. "That's what Tad Webster meant."

"Now you're being mysterious again," Brian said. "What does Spider Webster's brother, Tad, have to do with the situation? There isn't a better policeman in all Sleepyside than Spider," and he added, "or a better friend of the Bob-Whites of the Glen."

"That's true," Trixie agreed, "but he surely picked a goon for a younger brother. He saw me talking to Mr. Stratton and asked me what he had been saying to me."

"You didn't tell him, did you?" Diana asked. She didn't like Tad either.

"Of course I didn't. *He* told *me,* instead. Mr. Stratton had been questioning him, also, because Tad's president of the Hawks. Tad had the nerve to say that he thought the Hawks had a lot more reason for existence than the B.W.G.'s."

"Mr. Stratton said that?" Honey asked, her big hazel eyes widening.

"No, Tad did."

"They do have some good athletes in the Hawks," Mart said. He had been a Little Leaguer and could not quite make the Pony League when Tad did. "Tad can throw a curve as well as any pro."

"We're getting away from the subject again," Brian reminded Trixie.

"Oh, yes, thanks, Brian." Trixie was still breathless. "Tad told me that the vandalism and thievery—someone stole fifteen dollars out of Mr. Stratton's desk last night—had driven the board members and Mr. Stratton nearly crazy. Tad told me he thought they were out to get all clubs."

"You don't honestly believe that Mr. Stratton thinks the B.W.G.'s are breaking windows and looting desks and lockers, do you?" Jim asked. He and Brian found it difficult to rationalize some of Trixie's thinking.

"No, I don't. Oh, you all have me so confused I don't know what to think."

"You didn't just sit there and take what Mr. Stratton said, did you?" Mart asked. "Didn't you tell him about any of the *good* things the club has done?"

"I didn't, Mart, because those things are what make

the club secret, things like—well, like showing up Diana's phony uncle, and—"

"Helping me get away from my cruel stepfather," Jim said.

"And the time you and Honey saved little Sally Darnell's life—and catching Dapper Dick, the thief—" Mart started counting on his fingers. "Well, what did you tell him, Trixie?"

"I told him about how Jim is going to start a school for boys some day."

Big, red-haired, freckled Jim looked embarrassed. When his Great-uncle James Frayne died and left half a million dollars to his orphaned nephew, Jim had put it all in a trust fund dedicated to a school for orphan boys that he planned to open when he finished college.

"Did you tell him Brian is going to be the resident physician at my school?" Jim asked Trixie.

"Yes, I did. I told him, too, that Mart is going to take care of all the land around it when he finishes agricultural school."

"And that wasn't enough for him?" Diana asked.

"No, it wasn't. He said that was all far in the future. He thought it was 'splendid for you to want to help one another.'" Trixie touched the fingers of her hands together and rocked back on her heels in imitation of Mr. Stratton. "Then he spoiled it all by saying that he and the board would have a hard time believing that our little club could do anything for millionaires like the Wheelers and the Lynches."

"I wish—*how* I wish we didn't have any more money than anyone else," Honey moaned.

"I wish the same thing," said Diana.

"He doesn't know how wonderful and kind and generous you and your families are," Trixie said. "Anyway, money doesn't solve all the troubles people have."

"That's right," Honey agreed. "Mr. Stratton should talk to Miss Trask and she'd tell him what a different person the B.W.G.'s have made of me."

Miss Trask had been Honey's teacher when she was in private school. Now she lived in the Wheeler home and supervised it. It was she who insisted that Honey's mother and father send her to public school, outfit her in blue jeans for play, and let her do the things other girls her age were doing. Honey, who had been sickly most of her life, was now pink-cheeked and starry-eyed with health.

"He should know, too," Diana said, "how the B.W.G.'s gave my parents a whole new set of values.

We're lots more of a family since my mother and father discharged the butler, the nurses for my twin brothers and twin sisters, and half the maids. They thought when we first moved into this neighborhood that we'd have to live like millionaires. I guess we couldn't do it because we've really been poor most of our lives."

"We're getting away from the subject again," Brian warned. "What makes the situation so urgent now, Trixie?"

"The school board is having a meeting tonight—"

"And?"

"And they may very well tell us that we can't ever be a club again!"

"Our beautiful clubhouse that we've worked so hard to rebuild!" Diana sighed. She was the newest club member. She had felt pretty lonely before the B.W.G.'s had asked her to join them. "I used to look at you, Trixie, and your two older brothers, Brian and Mart, and Honey and her adopted brother, Jim, and think that nothing would ever make me quite as happy as to be asked to be a B.W.G. and now—"

"And *now,*" said Trixie, once more the efficient co-president of the club, "now we aren't going to go down without a fight."

"Most of what you have been saying has been

trying to read Mr. Stratton's mind." Jim was being practical. "Don't you think it would be a good idea if we were to talk to Mr. Stratton before that meeting this evening?"

"That's what I've been trying to tell you ever since I came in," Trixie said. "Mr. Stratton said he wanted all of us to come to his office at three thirty this afternoon."

"What do you think that means?" Diana asked. "A chance for us to save the club?"

"Trixie doesn't know that, Diana," Brian said. "*I* know this, however. If Jim and I don't get back into the kitchen pretty soon we'll be fired. That would make such a dent in the club's funds it would die a natural death."

"Let's meet here, then, at three twenty-five. We'll go to the principal's office together," Trixie said solemnly. "Jeepers, I forgot to eat my lunch. Not one of us ate anything. It's real trouble, sure enough, when we're too worried to eat."

The six members of the B.W.G.'s were a sad-faced lot. The club had been organized, in the first place, because the members' families lived out in the country near the little town of Sleepyside. All of them had to take the bus to school. The town boys and girls had many after-school activities which the bus travelers could not share.

Trixie, her brothers Brian, Mart, and little six-year-old Bobby lived at Crabapple Farm on Glen Road, two miles from Sleepyside.

On the western boundary of the farm, and just up the hill, Honey Wheeler, thirteen, lived with her parents and her adopted brother Jim, fifteen. Their home, Manor House, was a huge estate with acres of beautiful rolling lawn, a bird sanctuary and game preserve, a private lake, riding horses, and many servants.

Diana Lynch, thirteen, too, whose father had recently become a millionaire, lived in another large country estate. Her twin brothers and twin sisters were much younger.

In spite of the vast wealth of the others, the Beldens loved their white frame farm home best. Though their parents worked hard—their father had a position in the Sleepyside bank—they never lacked time to make their children's friends welcome.

The club members, whose secret whistle imitated a Bob-White's call, all wore red jackets which Honey had made, with "B.W.G." cross-stitched on the back.

They had remodeled the old gatehouse on the Wheeler estate, and now used it as a clubhouse. When they had first discovered it, it had been almost a ruin, set in a tangle of shrubs and vines. The B.W.G.'s had worked hard to rehabilitate it. The boys had done most of the repair work on the roof and interior. The girls had painted, made curtains, and helped clear the vines and shrubs away.

It was a rule of the club that all funds used in the work of the club had to be earned by the individual members. Honey's father and Diana's father would have financed the club for any amount, but the members did not want this. Trixie contributed five dollars a week which she earned helping her mother. Honey, who had learned to mend and sew at summer camps and private schools, earned the same amount as Trixie by doing mending. Diana was paid to help look after her little brothers and sisters. Mart did all the odd jobs he could find around the neighborhood. Jim and Brian, of course, worked in the school cafeteria.

As a group they had patrolled the game preserve before Mr. Maypenny, the present gamekeeper, had been employed. For this Mr. Wheeler had paid them the regular gamekeeper's wages.

Recently, too, when they had been at a dude ranch in Arizona for two weeks at Christmastime, they had substituted for the regular work crew who had left mysteriously. Diana's uncle, who owned the ranch, had paid them the same wages that he paid the regular employees.

Working together, planning together, playing together, the six had grown into a close-knit clan. They believed sincerely in the worthwhile objectives of the Bob-Whites of the Glen.

Surely nothing could destroy the club now.

Chapter 2
Trixie's Big Idea

"Don't you think I'd better leave my Bob-White jacket in my locker?" Trixie asked when they all met to go to Mr. Stratton's office.

"Why do you want to do that?" Mart asked.

"Because it was our jackets that seemed to bother him so much," Trixie said. "On second thought, I don't think I *will* take mine off. We haven't done anything wrong."

"It would too closely approximate appeasement," Mart said. "In the minds of the most erudite men in diplomatic circles, an attempt to placate is tacit acknowledgment of guilt." Mart tried out all his big words on the club members. Diana's puzzled violet-blue eyes widened. She even mixed up one-syllable words.

"Never mind, Diana," Brian said. "He probably doesn't know what the words mean himself. He reads the editorials in the *New York Times* and learns them by heart." Secretly Brian was proud of his younger brother.

"I don't see how any of you can laugh," Trixie said. "Here we are now at the judgment seat."

Six serious-faced young people went into the principal's office. Six chairs were drawn up facing Mr. Stratton's desk.

"Good afternoon," he said and smiled. "Now let me see, you are Brian Belden . . . and you, Martin Belden."

They nodded their heads.

"And Jim Frayne?"

"Yes, sir," Jim said.

"And Madeleine Wheeler." Honey winced at the unfamiliar name.

"Trixie Belden. Is Trixie a nickname?" he asked, his eyes twinkling.

"Not exactly," Trixie answered. She had been christened Beatrix, but people didn't have to know that. Her understanding mother had just called her Trixie when she enrolled for kindergarten.

"Last of all, Diana Lynch." Mr. Stratton straightened. His smile faded. "Now who is to be spokesman?"

"I am," said Trixie. Jim was co-president of the Bob-Whites, but Trixie usually did the talking because . . . well, because she was naturally chatty.

"Trixie, you have told me about the B.W.G. club and the reason for its being. I'm afraid it isn't enough. The board feels it must scrutinize closely the reason for any organization not sponsored directly by the school. It doesn't want secret societies to exist in Sleepyside schools, when clubs—really gangs—can be the source of so much trouble. With vandalism occurring in Sleepyside, we feel we *must* clamp down. And whatever ruling we make about secret clubs will affect the good ones as well as the bad."

"But the Bob-Whites of the Glen isn't a secret club," Jim said, "except when we try to do good, and we don't shout that to the world."

"That is to be commended," Mr. Stratton agreed. "The real fault seems to be that the work is carried on in too restricted a field."

"We can only do so much," Brian said. "And we do help people outside our own members. I can't talk about it, but we do."

"I think the members of the school board might consider a state or a national project," Mr. Stratton said.

"Creeps, we aren't the American Red Cross," Mart said in a low voice.

"I beg your pardon," Mr. Stratton said, "I didn't hear you."

"I meant, do you think we should be like the American Red Cross?" Mart, ashamed now, repeated.

"Nonsense!" Mr. Stratton said. "Of course everyone

helps the Red Cross. I'm afraid you don't grasp what I mean. I *can* say, though, and it is food for serious thought: The board feels very strongly that you must show a valid reason to continue to exist or, well, they didn't actually say so, but they meant that you will have to disband."

"We couldn't!" Trixie almost shouted.

"No, we couldn't," Diana echoed. "Why, Mr. Stratton, we'd do anything else in the world except give up the Bob-Whites."

Jim and Brian and Mart exchanged glances. Jim spoke for the trio. "I'm sorry, sir, but that is something we couldn't do. We think our club has a good purpose and we can't see why anyone should try to make us disband. We just couldn't break up our club."

"Even if refusal meant expulsion?" Mr. Stratton asked reluctantly.

"Not that!" Trixie gasped, her mind turning to what her mother and father would surely say. She squared her shoulders. "Is there *anything* we can do, Mr. Stratton?"

"I don't know," Mr. Stratton said sadly. "I'll try to explain to the board that the Bob-Whites are not a secret society in the true sense of the word, at least not the kind they deplore. If only you could have some really worthwhile project under way."

It was apparent that Mr. Stratton was not the nosy troublemaker Mart had labeled him; that he really was their friend.

"I *wish* we felt free to tell you some of the things the B.W.G.'s have done," said Honey. "Why just this Christmas we earned four hundred dollars out at a dude ranch and—"

"Honey!" Jim warned.

Honey covered her mouth with her hand. She had been so carried away she had almost told that they had given the money to the little Navaho hotel maid at the ranch to help pay for her father's operation.

While Honey had been talking, Trixie had wriggled around in her chair, impatiently waiting to have the floor. Now she jumped up. "I have a *wonderful* idea!" she said. "Mr. Stratton, could we please have just about fifteen minutes for a small conference?"

Mr. Stratton took out his watch. "Mercy, yes," he said. "I had an appointment at four fifteen, and it's nearly four thirty now. Just stay right here and talk things over. I'll be back at five."

Trixie, Honey, Diana, Brian, Jim, and Mart stood till he left the room. Then they pulled their chairs close around Trixie.

"Let's have it, Master Brain," said Mart. "I don't see

much ahead for the Bob-Whites but sabotage by the school board."

"Don't say that, Mart!" Diana cried and stamped her foot. "I know Trixie will think of something to get us out of this trouble."

"She can get us *into* more trouble than a bunch of Kilkenny cats," said Mart.

"And *out* of trouble, too," Jim said. "I'll never forget who saved me from the fire when my great-uncle's mansion burned."

"You'd have been a gone goose if she hadn't thought of a way out when Diana's phony uncle tried to kidnap both of you," Brian reminded Mart.

"That's right," Mart said shamefacedly. "She saved Bobby, too, when the copperhead snake bit him."

"Please . . ." Trixie begged.

"We could go on and on telling of things Trixie has done for us," Honey said, "even if she did get us into some bad situations, too. Right now, though, we have only a few minutes to think of something to keep the Bob-Whites from going out of existence. All right, Trixie, what's your idea?"

"How about something to help UNICEF, the United Nations International Children's Emergency Fund?" Trixie asked. Then she added dramatically,

"That would cover the whole world!"

"Say, Trixie, that really sounds like something," Mart said excitedly. "Just let the school board try to put the heat on us when we're doing something for the United Nations!"

"It isn't time for back-patting yet," Jim said slowly. "What does the Children's Fund do, Trixie?"

"I only know about a few things," Trixie said, "but they are almost miraculous."

"For instance?" Jim asked.

"Working with other organizations in the United Nations, UNICEF has trained nurses, doctors, teachers, technicians, in about eighty countries in the world, helping them to make use of their own resources. You see, it isn't just for today they are helping, but for years to come." Trixie's eyes shone as her idea unfolded.

"Can you tell us of some specific instance where the Fund has operated?" Mart was insistent. "Mr. Stratton will have to have facts to present to the board."

"Heavens, they already know about the Fund itself, because we've been donating to it for a long time," Trixie said. "For your information, though, I can tell you that in Nicaragua, for instance, the Fund has helped build dry-milk factories, so that milk could be manufactured in the flat dairy land, and transported burro-back over the mountains for children who have never even had a cup of milk in their lives."

"Trixie Belden, do you really mean they've never had a drop of milk before?" Honey was so tender-hearted her eyes filled with tears at the very thought.

"That's what I mean. In a lot of other non-dairy countries, too, such as Thailand, technicians sent out by UNICEF have been teaching people how to make milk from soy beans. First they taught them to grow, cultivate, and harvest soy beans."

"Food isn't all, either," said Brian. Because he was going to be a doctor, he was aware of the health needs of people in far-off countries. "Those nurses and doctors that UNICEF trains have helped people get rid of malaria, trachoma, tuberculosis, typhoid, diphtheria, and almost every crippling disease that has attacked undernourished children."

"That surely makes the little things we've been doing to help one another look pretty small," Diana said. "What can we do to raise money?"

"A bake sale?" Honey asked.

The boys threw up their hands and hooted.

"*You* could teach skiing," Diana told them.

"Heck, everyone around here knows how to ski," said Mart. "I wouldn't have any pupils."

"Well, *you* think of something then, smarty," Trixie said.

"Nobody would come to an amateur play we'd give," Honey said.

"We have them free all the time at school," said Brian. "No, it has to be something quite different, and something we can all help with. If it isn't, I don't think Mr. Stratton will consider it."

"Anything I can think of would take forever to raise any money," said Diana, "like baby-sitting, and reading to sick people, and . . . Trixie Belden, you've thought of something!"

"I have!" Trixie said exultantly. "I've exactly the right thing . . . an antique show!"

"A what?" Mart asked.

"An antique show!" Trixie repeated.

"How could we have an antique show?" Mart asked.

"Well, you know how it is, here in the East," Trixie said, the words falling over one another in her eagerness to explain. "*Everyone* is interested in antiques."

"Yeah, and everyone has them," Mart said woefully, thinking of the four-poster bed in his room at home, and comparing it with the neat bunk beds he had seen pictured in a magazine.

"Nobody ever has *enough* antiques," Trixie said.

"Anyhow, we'd exhibit some of the rare ones owned by people in the country around here, so other people could see them."

"We could charge admission!" Diana said breathlessly.

"Of course," Trixie said. "The big thing, though, would be to gather up old broken furniture from all around, repair it, refinish it, and sell it. The boys could do that."

"And what would *you* be doing in the meantime?" Mart asked.

"I'd make some rag dolls to sell." Honey answered instead of Trixie. "And some aprons."

"I don't know what I could do, but it sounds perfectly super, Trixie," Diana said.

"You and I can take our sleds and gather up a lot of small things—chairs, footstools, and little tables," Trixie said. "We can call on people to ask them to let us show their antiques, too. I think we could get Tom, your chauffeur, to pick up the bigger things, couldn't we, Honey?"

"I'm sure he'll help," Honey said.

"You and Diana can help sand the old furniture, too," Mart said. "Taking the old finish off is the worst part."

"We'd be glad to," Trixie said, so in love with the project she would agree to do anything.

"We can all put it over," Brian said, "but it's going to mean a lot of hard work because each of us has other chores at home."

"And extra schoolwork to make up for being away in Arizona," Trixie moaned. "It isn't impossible, though. Let's shake hands on it, Bob-Whites!"

They all shook hands solemnly.

"For goodness' sake keep your fingers crossed," Trixie went on. "I think I hear Mr. Stratton coming down the hall. He just *has* to let us do it. Just think, we'd be doing something to help all those children, and maybe save the Bob-Whites, too!"

Chapter 3
"The Winnah!"

The B.W.G.'s were busy with pencils and paper when Mr. Stratton came in.

"Well, it looks to me as though you've been doing some planning," he said. "You don't look nearly so dejected, either," he added.

"No, sir, we're not," Jim said. "We think Trixie has thought of something that may appeal to the board members. If you only approve of it we'll work real hard to make it a success."

"It isn't a question of *my* approval," Mr. Stratton said. "You know who the board members are, and how seriously they take their work. We have the finest schools in Westchester County. Sleepyside Junior-Senior High School is their special pride, and they are pretty much upset over the situation here just now. They've had a complaint, too, recently, from a source they respect, about possible secret societies here. They want the school to be everyone's school."

"But we've already told you that we started our club because we don't have a chance to work and play with others after school," Trixie said.

"The bus is right there waiting for us as soon as school is out," Diana reminded him. "We don't have any chance to be with the other kids."

Mr. Stratton smiled. "The meeting is to be held this evening, you know. Hadn't you better tell me of your club's plan, Trixie?"

In a forthright manner, without being dramatic, Trixie outlined the planned project of the Bob-Whites of the Glen. Her blue eyes grew big and serious as she told of the work of UNICEF; of how the B.W.G.'s hoped to contribute to the Fund through money received from an antique show; that it would mean hard work on their part, and how eager they were to help.

"You have presented a very good case for your club," Mr. Stratton told Trixie when she had finished talking. "The other club members seem to be just as inspired as you are."

"I didn't realize how much need there is to help children in oppressed parts of the world until Trixie told us of UNICEF," Jim said.

"Not any of us did," Honey added, "and even if we don't get to keep on with our club, we still all want to help, don't we?" She nudged Diana, and looked expectantly at Brian and Mart.

"I feel the same as Honey," Diana said.

"Me, too," Mart said. "I know a keen way to take off old varnish. I *like* to work on furniture."

"I'll do everything I can," Brian said. "I think we all owe you a vote of thanks, Mr. Stratton, for giving us this chance to work for UNICEF."

"It is *your* plan, not mine," Mr. Stratton reminded them. "And it is the board members, not me, who will give you your chance. I'll lay the whole matter before them. You may be sure they will be fair."

"They can't possibly know what it means to us," Trixie said sadly.

"I'll try to present *that* view of it to them, too," Mr. Stratton assured her. "Now I think you may be excused. I'll let you know tomorrow about the board's decision."

It was growing dark when the B.W.G.'s left the schoolhouse. The long low modern building was deserted except for the janitors. Street lights appeared one by one, casting early evening shadows on the banked snow on either side of the street. Cars hurried by carrying businessmen from commuter trains and from offices to homes.

The B.W.G.'s had been so intent on their problem that they hadn't been aware of the passing of time.

"Jeepers, it's almost six o'clock!" Brian said. "We'd better get on the phone and explain why we've been late."

"Moms will be sure something has happened," Trixie said. "We should have called her before. She always says that all she wants us to do is to let her know *where* we are, *what* we are doing, and *why.*"

"Tell her Regan will come for us in our station wagon," Honey said, "or Tom. I'll go now and call my home."

Regan was the Wheelers' groom. He looked after the five riding horses and the stables. He was much more than a groom. Because Honey's parents were away so much of the time, he helped Miss Trask look after the big house and estate, Honey and Jim, and, in fact, all the rest of the Bob-Whites and their brothers and sisters.

The Bob-Whites knew he would put aside whatever he was doing and come for them. Brian and Jim, though, in quick consultation, were not sure that was what they wanted him to do.

"Wait a minute, Honey," Jim called. Honey walked back to where the others were standing. The rest of the Bob-Whites looked at Jim, waiting to hear what he had to say.

"Can you stand it," he asked, "to wait till tomorrow

to find out what action the board members take?"

"Is there an alternative to our own disposition?" Mart asked, patting his mouth to cover an imaginary yawn.

"Oh, stop it, Mart," Brian said. "There is this alternative: We can stay in town till the meeting is over and go out to Mr. Stratton's house and ask him what the board decided."

"Why, yes!" Trixie cried. "Of course we can do that . . . that is, if our parents will let us. Let me see, we'd better call Regan first and be sure he can pick us up when the meeting is over. Then we can call our parents. Heavens, I've just thought of something. . . ."

"Run up a flag," Mart said, laughing, "Trixie's brain is working."

"Every once in a while it works," Trixie said. "How do you suppose the walks were shoveled at Crabapple Farm, Mart? Daddy will be home by now and he'll be furious at you and Brian."

"Seems to me this is the night you were supposed to take care of Bobby till Moms gets home from her Guild meeting," Mart remembered. "Won't you be in for a little parental ire yourself?"

"Miss Trask stopped by the school and took Bobby home with her," Honey said.

Trixie sighed in relief. "I guess it's up to you to call Daddy," she said to Brian. "He knows by now that something has delayed us."

"I'll tell him we'll get up early in the morning and shovel the snow," Brian said. "Here goes!"

Honey and Diana went inside the school, too, to use the public telephone in the vestibule.

"Another problem arises," Mart said, when they were together again. "A question of finances. We have to eat." He turned his pocket inside out. "I have exactly nothing."

"I have fifty cents," Trixie said, hunting in the pocket of her car coat.

"Think no more about it," Jim assured them. "We have a charge account at Wimpy's. Dad set it up for Honey and me in case of an emergency. We can fill up on hamburgers, French fried potatoes, and malts at least. Let's go."

"Saved!" Mart said.

Forgetting for a little while the dark cloud that filled their sky, the B.W.G.'s crowded into the narrow replica of a dining car.

Only one person was at the counter—Spider Webster.

"Well, if it isn't the prize member of the FBI and

her squad," Spider said as they filled the seats around him.

Trixie wrinkled her nose at him.

"Have you rounded up any crooks lately?" Spider asked.

"No, but I wish I could. There are some crooks just spoiling to be caught." Trixie was serious.

The man behind the counter waited.

"Two hamburgers all around," Jim said. "Is that all right, gang?"

They nodded.

"With everything," Mart added, "onions, catsup, tomatoes, relish—"

"And French fried potatoes," Jim added. "Heaps of them. I'm starved."

"We didn't eat a thing at noon," Honey explained. Their faces fell, remembering. "Chocolate malts, Mike," she told the counter man. "And hurry!"

"Now what's this about the crooks who need attention?" Spider wanted to know, moving the catsup bottle over to Trixie who sat next to him.

"Haven't you heard about all the things that have happened at Junior-Senior High?" Honey asked.

Spider's face sobered. "Why, yes, yes I have. We're working on it."

"The teachers seem to think it may be an inside job," Mart said.

Spider spoke nervously. "They do?" he asked. "The police haven't any clues so far as I know. I don't think they've ever thought it was any of the students, though."

Spider's brother, Tad, fourteen, was a freshman at Sleepyside High. Their father and mother were dead and Spider had tried to take over their place with Tad. The B.W.G.'s had some idea of how much Tad worried his brother, and it made them provoked. They didn't think Tad was really bad, but they did wish he would act his age.

Mart went on talking. "The teachers think it must be kids," he said. "You see, they do crazy things like some kids do."

"Like what?" Spider asked.

"Such things as upsetting desks, spilling waste-baskets, even breaking some of the windows. . . ."

"No looting?" Spider asked.

"Last night, yes," Mart answered. "Isn't that what you told us, Trixie?"

"Last night," Trixie said soberly, "someone stole some money from Mr. Stratton's desk, and a number of the lockers were broken open."

The look on Spider's face alarmed her when she said this. Suddenly she remembered a conversation she had overheard in the hall. Tad was telling another member of the Hawks that he had asked his brother Spider for ten dollars for some equipment they needed. Tad said his brother told him he didn't have the money. Could it be that Spider wondered if Tad might have found another way to get his hands on some money?

Spider's voice broke in on Trixie's puzzlement. "I suppose you kids think you can find the vandals, and that's why you're in town on a school night," he said sarcastically. "If so, you'd better go on home. That's a job for the police."

"That isn't the reason," Trixie said and told him of the threat to their club's existence. She told him, too, of the plan they had to try to save the club.

Tad came in while they were talking and heard Trixie telling about the proposed antique show. "Huh!" he sneered. "Who'd ever go to an old antique show? Why don't you have a boxing match?"

"Who'd do the boxing?" Spider asked.

"*I* would," Tad said. "I'd take on both Brian and Jim any day."

"What a long tail our cat has!" Mart jeered.

"Yes, and I'd take you on, too, squirt," said Tad,

doubling up his fists. "What makes you think people would be so crazy as to let you exhibit their valuable heirlooms? You take a lot for granted."

"We *know* people will help us when they find out our show is for UNICEF," Trixie said indignantly.

Spider looked at his watch and jumped to his feet. "I'm supposed to be out on Main Street," he said. "See you later. Come on, Tad."

Tad picked up his brother's unfinished Coke, gulped it down, swaggered after Spider. "See you later," he said. "Us Hawks want to see how the board jumps tonight, too."

Trixie looked through the window, saw Spider open his wallet and hand a bill to Tad. Then she heard the sputter of Spider's motorcycle.

"We want to be careful not to mention how valuable some of the antiques are that we will show," Trixie said. "It might give people ideas about stealing them."

"There you go," Jim said, "wearing your Moll Dick badge again. Forget it, Trixie. Here comes the food."

Mike put the hot fragrant plates before them.

"Is there anything in the world better than a hamburger?" Jim asked. "More French fried potatoes, please, Mike."

"I could eat a boiled owl I'm so hungry," Trixie said.

"What do you suppose made Spider act so odd?"

"I didn't notice anything queer," Brian said.

"I didn't either," said Diana.

"Then it must have been my imagination," Trixie said and bit into her juicy sandwich.

"Boy, do you have a supply of that!" Mart said.

"Maybe I do have imagination, Mart, but I don't talk with my mouth full," Trixie retorted. "How are we going to kill time till that meeting is over?"

"We have plenty of homework to do. We could go over to the library and I could help you with your math, Trixie." Brian was the most earnest one in the group. He always did his homework.

"Jeepers, I couldn't put my mind on anything till we find out what the board is going to do. I know I'm the one who needs homework most, Brian; you don't need to look at me like that. My math is getting worse every day. But could any one of you do justice to lessons now?"

They shook their heads—even Brian.

"Then I vote for an early movie."

"*If* we have the price," Mart said. "Someone will have to stake me."

They hunted in pockets, poured out their contributions, passed the collection down to Jim. "It's more than enough," he said. "There's even some left for popcorn."

The movie was a stirring western. Honey, who was timid, and easily frightened, moved closer to Trixie. Absent-mindedly Trixie patted Honey's arm to reassure her, her own eyes glued on the screen, her spirit far away, galloping madly across the prairie.

Finally the "bad guys" were rounded up, the cartoon flickered to an end, and the Bob-Whites were out on the street again.

"Five minutes after ten," Jim said, turning his watch face up under the light. "It must be nearly time for the meeting to be over."

"How far is it to Mr. Stratton's house?" Honey asked, shivering. She hadn't liked the movie.

"Just around the corner, Sis. Are you cold?" Jim asked and pulled a wool scarf out of his pocket to wrap around Honey's shoulders.

"Not cold," she answered. "Those western pictures frighten me."

"How you could have followed Trixie into some of the tight spots she's led you into, I'll never know," Mart said.

"I didn't know about them until I was into them." Honey sighed. "When I did know I'd have been more frightened to have her go on alone."

They walked along briskly. There was only a faint

light in the upstairs room of Mr. Stratton's house. The family must have gone to bed.

"We'll have to be quiet," Trixie whispered. "Oh, gleeps, there's Tad. Warn him to be quiet, Brian. I'm freezing. I hope Mr. Stratton isn't too long getting here."

Tad came up to them, swelled his chest out, and beat on it with his two fists to keep warm.

"The meeting was just letting out as I passed the school," he whispered. "If the board thinks they can put the Hawks out of business they'll have another think coming. We'll just go under cover."

"You couldn't do that," Diana said.

"Oh, we couldn't?" Tad jeered. "Just watch. No, honestly I sure hope we can carry on as we are. Say, Mart," his voice grew louder, then Trixie shushed him, "we've got the sweetest thing at bat you ever saw, in the Pony League now—Matt Devlin."

"Why, good evening!" Mr. Stratton's surprised voice interrupted Tad. "This is pretty late for you to be in town on Thursday night. Of course I know why you stayed."

"Yes, we couldn't possibly wait till tomorrow. We can't possibly wait another minute!" Trixie caught Mr. Stratton's arm as he reached to open his door. "Tell us, won't you?"

"Yeah," Tad said. "The Hawks want to know, too."

"I'm sorry it's too late to ask you to come in," Mr. Stratton said. "Here it is, straight from the shoulder. I won't tell you of the discussion that came first. The members of the board were indignant about what has been going on at our junior-senior high school."

"Did you tell them we didn't have anything to do with it?" Trixie asked.

"No, because I don't think they were thinking in specific terms about anyone. When I had an opportunity I explained how the Bob-Whites came into existence. Then I outlined the project you have in mind for UNICEF. . . ."

"And?" Trixie could wait no longer.

"Well, they didn't say outright that you would have to disband."

They all sighed with relief.

"They did say, however," Mr. Stratton continued, "that you would be placed on probation."

The girls groaned. The boys shuffled their feet.

"Until," the principal went on, "until they could appraise the outcome of the antique show. So, boys and girls, it's up to you. If you make a great success of the show, and the members of the board see how well you can work together to accomplish great good—they *did* think that raising money for UNICEF is very worthwhile—then they will consider allowing your club to continue to function."

"Hurray!" they cried in unison.

A window went up upstairs. "Jeepers, we're sorry," Trixie called up to Mrs. Stratton, whose head appeared. "But thanks a million times, Mr. Stratton. We know it was the way you talked to them that won them over. Thanks!"

"Well now, thank *you*," Mr. Stratton said and reached again for the doorknob.

"Say, how about the Hawks, sir?" Tad's voice was low, most unusually humble.

"The Hawks?" Mr. Stratton repeated. "Oh yes, the board members said right away that they could continue—good for the health of the members—good for the school—yes, now good night!"

He went into the house.

Tad, cocky again, and triumphant, shook his clasped hands over his head. "The winnah!" he said and dashed away.

"That's what he thinks," Mart said, as the group followed Tad up the street. Regan would be waiting for them at the drugstore on Main Street.

"Let's not bother about what Tad thinks," Jim said. "Right, Trixie?"

"Right, Jim!" *What a co-president he is!* Trixie thought.

Out in the street they went, hand in hand, heads up, singing at the tops of their voices.

Nothing could stop them now!

Chapter 4
Treasures in the Attic

"Here comes Reddy again!" Bobby shouted. "He'll get right in front of my sled! Down, Reddy! Please go back home, Reddy!"

Trixie had taken her little brother out to the hill behind Crabapple Farm to slide. Reddy, their Irish setter, wanted to go sliding, too. That is, he wanted to do anything Bobby wanted to do. It was plain to be seen which one of the children he liked best. Maybe it was because Bobby had more time to play with him.

"Go back home, Reddy!" Trixie ordered. "Bad dog!"

"He's not a bad dog. He's a good dog. He minds me," Bobby said. "Sit down, Reddy! Sit down and watch me slide! Now, mind!"

Reddy obediently settled himself on his haunches at the top of the hill. He watched as Trixie settled her brother on the sled, then pushed him on his way. Reddy did want so much to play. He whimpered to try to tell them so.

Down the hill Bobby went. Trixie ran along behind him.

The next time Reddy did not sit still when Bobby started down. Instead, he ran back and forth barking till the little boy pushed off.

Then Reddy settled himself on his haunches on the icy slide and went down after Bobby.

At the bottom of the hill he jumped to his feet and barked furiously. "I can slide, too," he seemed to say.

Again and again they went down the hill; Bobby, then Reddy, sliding, and Trixie running along beside them.

"This is the last time this morning," Trixie finally called as Reddy, tired of sliding, raced after Bobby.

"Reddy and me don't like last times," Bobby said when Trixie caught up with him at the bottom of the hill. She put his sled in the garage and they went into the house.

"Reddy slided downhill, too," Bobby told his mother, "but Trixie only pushed me eleven times."

"Oh, Moms, it was lots more than that," Trixie said. "You should have seen Reddy. He sat down and slid down the hill on his haunches!"

"I shut him up twice when he tried to join you, then I gave up. I didn't know Reddy could coast, too. And, Bobby, no matter how many times Trixie pushed you, you were out long enough." She gave Bobby a piece of the apple she was paring. "Trixie has to dust the house for me while I make this pie—I mean these pies. The way my family can dispose of pies is a mystery to me."

"You shouldn't make such good ones, Moms," Trixie said. "If I made a pie it would last two weeks, and then we'd have to throw it out."

"I know of a way to change that," her mother said, her pink cheeks flushed with the heat of the oven. "Next Saturday, instead of pushing Bobby on his sled, you may have a lesson in pie-baking."

"I'll never in a million years be able to cook as you do," Trixie said. "We have the best food in all the world in our house—tomatoes, corn, pickles, the things you canned from our garden last summer."

"Don't forget that you and the boys kept the gardens cultivated and gathered all the vegetables and fruit for me. Everyone works in this house."

"Yes, we do, but you know, Moms, we aren't going to be able to do much around the house until after the antique show. I hope we make a lot of money to send to UNICEF. Wasn't it wonderful of the board members to give us a chance to keep our club?"

"I suppose it was. I've never known what they objected to in the first place. I think the Bob-Whites have done some pretty wonderful things. I'm proud of you.

I *don't* like all the sleuthing you do. Maybe you've had enough of that now."

"Maybe so. I won't have time for it now."

"You get mixed up in so many things, Trixie." Mrs. Belden sighed. "I wish you weren't such a tomboy. You looked so pretty when you dressed up every day and pretended you were impressed with that cousin of Honey's."

"That drip!"

"Trixie! Watch your language!" Mrs. Belden opened the oven door, slid a pie inside, then started to roll the crust for the next pie.

"Even Honey thinks he's one," Trixie said. "Moms, we have a terrible amount of work to do to get ready for our antique show. I don't even know where to begin."

"I was talking to one of the members of the Garden Club this morning," Mrs. Belden said. "She told me she'd let you have her two Chinese Chippendale chairs to show."

"That's super!" Trixie cried. "I'll personally guarantee they won't be scratched in any way. Regan and Tom said they'd pick up all the things the day before the show. The big problem is where to hold it."

"Didn't your father tell you?" Mrs. Belden asked. "I remember, now, you weren't awake when he left for the bank. He said he was sure he could arrange for you to use that storeroom the bank has for rent, the one just across the street from the clothing store. It's right on Main Street."

"Christopher Columbus!" Trixie shouted. "Right on Main Street! Wait till I tell the others."

"You can tell Honey and Diana soon. They're coming down the hill from the Manor House. The boys took Brian's car into Sleepyside to have the brakes tightened. I wish Brian had snow tires on that old car."

"He doesn't need them. You should see the way we get Brian's jalopy out of a snowbank. We all get out and push. We can almost lift it when it gets stuck. We don't have any money for tires even if we did want them. Every cent we have will go into preparation for the show."

Bobby opened the door to Honey and Diana.

"Good morning, Mrs. Belden," they chorused. Then without waiting for her to answer, "Trixie, just wait till you hear what we have to tell you!"

"Let me tell you *my* news first," Trixie said. "Daddy's bank is almost certain to let us use that old storeroom where Mr. Bennington's electric shop used to be. It's right on Main Street!" she added, doing a little *cha cha* step.

"That makes the show as good as a complete, entire, super-duper success right now!" Honey said and hugged Trixie.

"Now let me tell you *my* surprise," Diana said. "So we can work on the used furniture, my daddy is going to give us an oil burner he used to use in the apartment over our garage. He will have it remodeled and installed in the clubhouse."

"Oh, no, he won't," Trixie said.

Diana opened her big eyes in astonishment. "Why not?"

"Diana, please don't look like that," Trixie said. "I meant you know we can't just take it as a gift."

"My daddy won't be using it at all," Diana said. "Don't be so particular, Trixie."

"I'm not the only one who is particular, and you know it," Trixie said. "It's Jim. Jim is so con—cons—"

"Conscientious," her mother supplied.

"Thanks, Moms. Jim thinks we should be careful to keep our rule: Earn everything we use for the club. I think Jim's right. He's always right."

Mrs. Belden smiled a little. Trixie's face flushed. "Well he *is* always right," she insisted. "Maybe, though, we could compromise, if your father really isn't going to use the oil burner, Diana."

"He isn't," Diana said. "He was going to give it to anyone who'd take it away."

"In that case, maybe Jim will think we can take it. We'll have to pay to have it repaired and installed, or," Trixie added, "I'd not be surprised if Jim and Brian could repair it and install it themselves. With some help from Regan, maybe."

"Now for *my* news," Honey said. "Regan is going to run an electric cord out from the stable to the clubhouse. Then we can have lights in the evening to work on the used furniture. Think how much longer we can work."

Trixie spun around the room, her eyes dancing. "Isn't it wonderful how everyone is helping?" she sang.

"That isn't all," Honey continued. "My mother said she was just about ready to clear out the attic and send all the odds and ends, as she called them, to some charity."

"All those beautiful, beautiful things in your attic?" Trixie cried. "I don't know any better charity than—"

"UNICEF, of course," Honey said. "Mother doesn't think the things are so beautiful. She told Jim and me this morning that we could have anything we wanted from that one big room over the upstairs library."

"Oh!" Trixie's face fell. "I've never been in that room. I thought she meant that beautiful furniture you used to have in your city home that she has stored in the attic. That was a silly thing to think," Trixie added.

"Some of the things in the other attic room are almost as pretty," Honey said. "They're older, and our show *is* an antique show. Of course they have to be glued here and there, and stained. Maybe some of the chairs have to be recovered. Why don't we go and look at them? I've only looked through the cubbyhole door, myself."

"I have to dust the house first," Trixie said. Her mother looked at her in amazement to think she had remembered.

"We'll help you, won't we, Diana? Jim's waiting for us at the house," Honey said. "Where are Brian and Mart?"

"In town with Brian's jalopy getting it fixed," Trixie said. "Maybe they will be here by the time we finish dusting."

"They are here now," Bobby announced. He had just opened the back door to ask his mother for a cooky. "Brian's car sounds so smooth now—just listen!"

They listened as Brian whirled the car around and backed it into the garage. It did not sound much louder than a cement mixer. The girls, hurrying around the house to finish the dusting, thought it sounded wonderful.

They loved Brian's old car almost as much as he did.

"Is there anything the boys have to do for Daddy?" Trixie asked, gathering the dustcloths and putting them in the broom closet.

"No," her mother answered. "This is one Saturday they haven't a thing to do. I mean outside of regular chores. They were going to wash the station wagon but it's too cold a day for that."

"Then may we go over to the Manor House and explore the attic? Did you hear that, Brian?" she asked her brother. "And Mart? There are some pieces of old furniture and other things in the Wheeler attic that Mrs. Wheeler said we could have for our show. Shall we go over and explore the attic now?"

"What's keeping us?" Mart asked and picked his little brother up and put him on his shoulder.

"Me, too?" Bobby asked.

"I'm afraid not today, lamb," Trixie said. "We're going to be pretty busy."

"Let him come, too," Honey said. "Miss Trask will read to him, or Regan will take him out to his apartment over the stable."

"Gee whiz, thanks, Honey," Bobby said and struggled down from Mart's shoulder.

"Mrs. Belden, if you don't mind, Miss Trask said to

ask you if they could all stay for lunch. She said it would just be hot dogs. May they?"

"I think so. Trixie, take Bobby up to his room and change his shirt, please. It seems as though the Belden children are always eating at your house, Honey."

"We come here more often, Mrs. Belden. Mother has all your recipes in a box at home, but she says Cook never makes them taste as good as you do."

"If I looked as pretty as your mother does," Mrs. Belden answered, "I'd never put a foot inside the kitchen."

"There isn't a movie actress who can hold a candle to you, Moms," Mart said and kissed her.

"Flattery will get you nowhere," his mother said, blushing. "Try to be home by four o'clock, all of you. Your father will be here then. He's going to bring that film we took at home on Christmas when you were at the dude ranch."

"We'll try to be on time, Moms. Do you know," Trixie put her arm around her mother, "that was one thing we could hardly stand—being away from Crabapple Farm at Christmas."

At the Manor House Regan met Bobby and took him by the hand to go to his apartment.

"Tell me my riddle," Bobby begged. "You always tell me good riddles."

"What has three keys but can't open locks?" Regan asked, his freckled face amused.

"That's a hard one," Bobby said. "It's not my skate key . . . it's not our door key . . . what's the answer, Regan?"

"A zoo. It has a mon*key*, a don*key*, and a tur*key*," Regan said. "Tell the other kids good-by, Bobby."

Honey led the Bob-Whites up the two flights of stairs to the attic. They had to go through a trap door to get into the room over the library. Cobwebbed boxes and furniture were stacked around the room. One light hung from the ceiling, sending weird shadows into all corners.

Trixie tingled with excitement. *It's the same setting, almost exactly,* she thought, *as the one in* Kidnaped for Ransom.

"I've never been inside this room before," Honey said. "I think most of the things must have been here when Daddy bought the house."

"Just look at this table!" Mart exclaimed. "It's cherry or I'll miss my guess. This is valuable, Honey, and here's its twin! Do you think your mother meant that we could have anything in this room?"

"That's what she told me," Honey answered.

Mart, excited, carried the two tables through the trap door to the hall. "This is the first installment," he said.

Trixie's head was deep in a big trunk she pulled open. "It's full of old costumes," she said. "The little theater in Sleepyside will pay a lot of money for these or . . . say, I think we'd better keep them and rent them to *all* the drama groups. We'd make more money that way. Look at this, what do you suppose it opens?"

Trixie held up a small key. There was a tag attached to it. "This is queer," she said and turned the tag face up so they could see it. On it were these little acrobatic figures in different postures:

"Do you suppose it says something?" Honey picked up the key and its tag and took it over under the light. "Did you ever see anything like this before?" she asked.

"It's probably some kind of a code," Mart said. "It's neat. I'll bet some kid did that a long time ago."

"Right," Jim said. "More than likely, though, it doesn't mean a thing."

"Maybe not," Trixie agreed, then slipped it in the pocket of her sweater. "What are you making such a fuss about, Brian?"

Brian had found an old sword, and rubbed it against his blue jeans to brush off the dust.

"Say, Jim, take a look at this," he said. "Could these be gold ornaments on the hilt?"

"Why don't you ask me?" Mart asked. "I'm an authority on swords. It's a samurai. There should be a dagger to match. They come in pairs."

The boys hunted around on the floor. "Here it is! It's a beauty!"

"The samurai were military guards at the mikado's palace way back in feudal days in Japan," Mart recited, sure of his subject. "They were the only ones allowed to wear the two swords."

"They had a pleasant way of using them," Jim said.

"They did," Mart agreed. "When the honor of a samurai was questioned, even ever so faintly, he had the great privilege of plunging this short dagger into his abdomen to end his life."

"Then his best friend, who bent over watching to see that he did the job neatly," said Brian, "would slice off his head with this long sword to be sure the dagger did its work."

"Don't talk about things like that," Honey said, her face white. "It makes me sick. Let's leave these old swords here. Nobody will want them."

"You're wrong, Honey," Brian said. "When I went to New York with Dad before Christmas I saw a Japanese sword in the gift department of a store. It wasn't as old as this one . . . at least I don't think it was . . . but the price on it was over a hundred dollars."

"I still don't like them," Honey said.

"It's history, though, Honey," Trixie said. "Whoopee, look at these old masks! This one—why, I believe it's a Garuda bird. Do you remember that Balinese dance we saw on TV out at the ranch?"

Mart picked up the mask, ran his hand down the long beak of the Garuda bird, with its serrated teeth. "I remember," he said. "A man wore one in the Balinese shadow play. Someone who lived here before must have traveled in the Far East and picked up these masks and swords."

Just then Celia, the Wheelers' pretty maid who had married Tom, the chauffeur, pushed a tray ahead of herself through the trap door. "Mrs. Wheeler said to bring these sandwiches up to you," she said and put a tray of hot dogs on an old trunk.

"Tom is bringing the milk," she added. "Bobby is

having his lunch with Regan. If you need anything more," she said to Jim, "just come down to the kitchen."

After they had finished their sandwiches they selected the articles they wanted to use.

"Let's carry this loot over to the clubhouse and get busy right away," Mart said enthusiastically. "Diana, you and Trixie can start to sand one of the gate-leg tables when we get there. If they're really cherry, we'll get a neat price for them. Come on, girls. Each one take a cooky jar. Jim, a table for you, and you, Brian, the mirror. Wait till you see the mirror with a new coat of gilt on the frame. I'll take the Indian."

Aside from the two gate-leg tables they took a tobacco shop Indian figure with some of its original paint, a Windsor armchair, a table that might turn out to be a Pembroke, a framed mirror, a brass coal hod, two brown crackled cooky jars, and a model of an old whaling ship, the *Oswego of Hudson.*

They stopped in the Manor House living-room to thank Mrs. Wheeler.

"Oh, that old stuff," she said. "You'll never find anyone who will want to buy it."

"You'd be surprised, Mrs. Wheeler," Mart said. "I'd like to place a bet that you buy one of your own things back when you see our show."

"That would surprise me very much," she said, laughing. "Is that an old Bennington jar you are carrying, Diana? I wonder where it came from."

"Do you see what I mean?" Mart asked impudently. "Do you want to buy it back now?"

Chapter 5
The Acrobatic Alphabet

When Trixie and her brothers went home for dinner, they were dusty and tired. They were so excited, however, that words piled on top of one another when they tried to tell their mother and father what had happened at the Manor House, of the wonderful things they had found there.

"That's enough about your afternoon, now," Mrs. Belden interrupted. "Take showers, all of you. Trixie, please help Bobby. Change to robes and slippers. You may eat your dinner in robes and get to bed early. Run along, now," she insisted as they kept on talking. "When we are at dinner we can hear all about it."

Later, when they were at the table, and grace had been said, Bobby shouted, "I'm first! Regan told me a good riddle."

"Let's hear it, son," Mr. Belden said.

"He told me two riddles," Bobby said. "This is the funniest one. What has ten letters and starts with—what is it, Trixie?" Bobby asked.

"It starts with G-A-S, remember?"

"Oh, yes, what is it, Moms? Daddy? You give up?"

Mr. Belden scratched his head and thought.

Mrs. Belden put her head in her hands and thought.

"We give up, Bobby," they said.

"Brian's jalopy!" Bobby said triumphantly and laughed till he almost choked.

"Bobby's a clown," Brian said. "The real answer is 'automobile.' Look here, Dad, at what I found in the attic."

Brian and Mart stood over their father's chair while he examined the swords. "This one looks just like the one we saw in New York," he said. "Yes, I think you made quite a find, Brian. Are you sure, you and Mart, that Mrs. Wheeler wanted to give them to you!"

"Sure thing," Mart answered. "She gave us some other keen things we found, too." He told his parents about the beautiful cherry-wood tables.

"I found a crazy-looking thing," Trixie said and produced the key and the tag with its acrobatic figures.

"It's a code of some kind, I'm sure," Mr. Belden said. "I think I saw something like it a long time ago."

"Can't you possibly remember, Daddy?" Trixie asked. "Maybe it would tell us something important."

"It looks more to me like some child's idea of a joke," Mrs. Belden said. "It probably doesn't mean a thing. All

Trixie needs," she said to her husband, "is something like this to start her off with a bloodhound. Forget it, Trixie. You'll have all you can possibly do, all of you, to get that furniture fixed up for your show. I don't see how you can possibly find time to repair any more than just the things you found in the Manor House attic."

"We have lots more promised to us," Mart said. "We'll have the best antique show Sleepyside ever saw."

"I don't doubt that," Mr. Belden said. "Right now I think you'd all better go to bed. You've been yawning, and look at Bobby. He's asleep with his head on the table."

"I'll help Moms with the dishes first," Trixie said.

"We'll put Bobby to bed," Brian said. "Come on, fella!" He lifted the little boy in his arms and went up the stairs, followed by Mart.

The next morning the boys were off for the clubhouse early. Jim had agreed that they could accept the oil heater and he and Brian were helping to install it. At the same time Regan, with an electrician who had been engaged to put in some new light switches in the Manor House, was going to run a feed wire to the clubhouse.

After Trixie hurried through the dusting she tossed the dustcloth in the broom closet in the kitchen. "I'm going over to Honey's house," she told her mother. "I want to look for something in the attic."

"*After* you pick up that dustcloth from where you threw it," her mother said. "And *after* you give the furniture in the living-room, the dining-room, and the study a good dusting, not just show the furniture to the dustcloth."

"Oh, Moms, I never have a chance to do anything I want to do. What's the matter with the way the furniture looks?" Trixie picked up the dustcloth and stamped into the living-room. Then, before she had dusted a thing she ran back penitently to her mother and gave her a quick hug.

"I'm so selfish," she said. "How do you ever put up with me, Moms?"

"Oh, maybe because I happen to love you," her mother said. "Never mind, Trixie, I remember when I was thirteen years old. Finish the dusting, then run along to Honey's."

Diana, summoned from her big home high on a hill, was at the Manor House when Trixie arrived. They rushed up the stairs to the attic, climbed through the trap door to the cubbyhole, put the key and the mysterious tag on top of an old trunk, and started to explore.

They looked under and around everything in the room: broken old ladders, discarded light fixtures, a three-legged hobby horse, storm windows, screens that needed repairing, discarded clothing packed in boxes. Trixie even rummaged through the boxes of clothing. They found an old chest filled with checkers and chess men, but the key with the strange figures didn't fit the keyhole.

They did find some very old toys that had been put up high in the rafters. There was an old Punch and Judy theater with Punch, quite tattered and worn, leaning over the door holding his big stick. There was a Sleeping Beauty doll minus her long golden hair. There were three plaster figures of the seven dwarfs.

"We can paint these and dress them in some new clothes," Honey said. "They'll be as good as new."

"Let's stop hunting for anything that key fits," Diana said. "We could hunt from now until the Fourth of July and never find it. It's probably been thrown out long ago. Let's take some of these old *St. Nicholas* magazines over under the light and look at them!"

Diana picked up two bound volumes of the magazine and carried them to the middle of the room. "My grandmother had some of them in *her* attic," Diana said. "Did you ever try to work any of the puzzles? Here, let's turn to the puzzle pages."

The girls sat on the floor inside the cubbyhole, the bound magazines in their laps.

"This one is way back in 1884," Diana said, opening the red cloth-bound book.

"Heavens, that was before the United States was born," Trixie said.

"Not quite," Honey laughed. "I thought you were better in history than math."

"See if you can answer this one, if you're so smart," Trixie said, her face red. "It's an easy charade, or so it says."

"Not any of the puzzles in *St. Nicholas* were easy," Diana said. "I guess people were smarter then."

"Try this anyway," Trixie said.

"Men hunt my *first,* then *second* my *first* in order to obtain my *whole.*"

"It must be something people hunt," Honey said. "Ducks . . . no; geese . . . no; rabbits . . . no; wolves . . . no. What is it, Trixie?"

"I don't know myself. I'll have to look it up in the answers. They're given the month following. Let me see . . . it's *sealskin!* You hunt *seal,* don't you see, then *skin* the *seal,* and you have *sealskin.* Say, look at this other page, would you? Jumpin' Jupiter! It's the acrobats, the whole alphabet! Where's that tag?"

Spread over a page in the old *St. Nicholas* magazine there was a group of dancing, tumbling little stick men, each posture representing a letter of the alphabet.

"Let me see now," Trixie said. "Let's compare the tag. This is *K;* here is an *E,* and then *Y.* That first word is *Key.* "

Quickly Trixie spelled out the rest of the message on the tag. Transcribed, it read: *Key to Riches.*

Trixie was so excited her hands were shaking. "It's a fortune!" she shouted. "I know it is. Come on!"

She jumped up and let the book tumble to the floor. "Let's start hunting!"

"We've covered every inch of this place," Diana said. "There isn't anything here that the key will fit. How do you know what we are hunting for is in the attic?"

"It *has* to be," Trixie said.

"Stand up here on this ladder," Honey said. "Reach up into the rafters, back of the Punch and Judy show. Isn't there something there?"

Trixie reached, almost fell off the ladder, brought out an old broken pull toy. Her face fell. "There's not another thing here," she said and climbed down.

Together the girls moved out all the old screens and storm windows, hunted over every inch of floor they had covered before, looked through the boxes of old

The Stick-man Code

clothes again till there was only one thing left, a chest that stood under the window in the closet next to the chimney.

"We hunted through that before, Trixie," Diana said.

"Let's hunt again," Honey cried and she and Trixie drew out armload after armload of clothes long packed in moth balls.

When she reached the bottom of the chest Trixie was so exasperated and disappointed she felt like crying. She slammed down the lid of the old chest and kicked it so hard it banged against the chimney, loosening several bricks that fell to the floor.

"Jeepers, I'm sorry, Honey," Trixie said. "Your mother will think this is terrible." She picked up a brick, started to replace it in the chimney, then stopped. Her eyes grew as round as robins' eggs. "Will you look at this?" she asked Honey and Diana. They put their heads close to hers.

Back of where the bricks had been there was an open space, and tucked cozily inside it was an old doll's trunk.

Dazed, Trixie pulled it out, put it on the floor, inserted the key in the lock, turned it, and all three girls fell to their knees to look.

Chapter 6
A Musical Mystery

"It's fantastic!" Trixie said.

"Yes," Diana echoed. "But what is it?"

"Since this is your house," Trixie said to Honey, "you lift it out and we'll see what it is."

Gently Honey lifted the treasure out and set it on the floor. It settled with a delicate tinkle.

"A music box!" they cried in unison.

The intricately carved and fashioned gold box showed no trace of tarnish. The gold was as bright as new. On the lid, under a garland of vines and arched trees, a little man and woman stood, dressed in court clothes of the time of Louis XVI.

"See if you can wind it," Honey said.

When Trixie turned the key on the bottom of the box the little figures danced daintily round and round to the tune of a Viennese waltz.

Completely charmed, the three girls sat and watched and listened, until the flute-like tune fluttered to a close.

"It's the most beautiful music box!" Honey said.

"And a jewel box, too," Trixie cried. "It opens!" She

lifted the lid and little drawers popped out all around the inside edges.

"There's something in one of the drawers!" Diana cried. "It's a ring!"

"*Two* rings!" Trixie announced. "Two exquisite rings," she added, awed.

"This one is an emerald," Honey said and slipped it on her finger.

"This one is a ruby," Diana said. "But it's a man's ring!"

"I think we had better take the jewel box downstairs and show it to your mother," Trixie declared solemnly.

Mrs. Wheeler was sitting at the piano in the music room, lightly strumming the keys. She looked up as the three excited girls burst into the room. Honey held the box in her hands and extended it to her mother.

"Don't tell me you've found a treasure in the attic," Mrs. Wheeler said, smiling. "In all mystery stories they always find treasures in the attic . . . why you *did!*" she exclaimed. "What is that lovely thing?"

Honey wound the box, set it tinkling, and put it on the piano. The dancing figures circled, their tiny feet moving in exact time to the music.

"It's beautiful," Mrs. Wheeler said. "It is lovely enough to have been made by Cellini! You *never* found that in the attic!"

"We *did!*" Honey said. "Yesterday we found the key. It fits an old doll trunk. See the key and the tag? The little figures were so mysterious Trixie couldn't be satisfied until she investigated it. Then we found that page in *St. Nicholas* with the alphabet."

"I don't believe Scotland Yard could have done a better piece of detective work," Honey's mother said.

"Then the bricks fell down and we found the doll trunk," Honey went on.

"I'm sorry about the bricks," Trixie said. "Not only the doll trunk, but . . . Honey, open the music box and show her what we found on the inside."

"This is serious," Mrs. Wheeler said when she saw the rings. "The box itself is priceless—and now the rings! I don't know what to think. Who *could* have put them in that doll trunk?"

"Could it have been the people who lived here before we came?" Honey asked.

"That's possible," her mother said. "That's it, of course. I have the family's number someplace. Their name was Spencer. When their two daughters grew up and married, they went to live in New York and we bought Manor House. I'll go and look for the phone number in my desk."

When Mrs. Wheeler came back with her address book, the girls, Honey holding the jewel box, went to the telephone room off the hall to listen to the conversation.

It seemed hard to make Mrs. Spencer understand. Mrs. Wheeler took the musical jewel box from Honey's hands and described it in detail.

"Are you sure?" Mrs. Wheeler said. "But you built the house. No one lived here but you until we bought it. It doesn't belong in *our* family."

"That's a mystery for your detective agency," she said to Honey and Trixie as she hung up the receiver. "Mrs. Spencer never even heard of the musical jewel box. She said neither she nor her husband ever had ruby or emerald rings. She doesn't even *like* emeralds!"

"Maybe the police have a record of the jewel box having been stolen," Trixie suggested. "You could call Sergeant Molinson and ask him."

"You call him if you know him," Mrs. Wheeler said.

"If I did he'd hang up before he'd listen to me," Trixie said, smiling. "He doesn't like amateur detectives."

"Then I'll call him," Mrs. Wheeler said.

She held the receiver a short distance from her ear so the girls could hear the conversation.

"Don't tell me those kids are mixed up in another mystery," the sergeant said. "What did you say about jewels?"

Mrs. Wheeler described the jewel box and the rings. "The emerald ring is valuable, I know. No one in our family ever saw the jewel box."

"Why don't you call the people who owned the place before you?" Sergeant Molinson asked.

Patiently Mrs. Wheeler told him she had done this, and that Mrs. Spencer never had heard of the jewel box either.

"I called you to see if it had ever been reported stolen," she went on.

"Hold the line, please. I'll look it up," Sergeant Molinson said. "I don't remember anything about it. Just a minute."

"He isn't very co-operative," Mrs. Wheeler said, aside, to the girls, as she waited while the sergeant searched the records.

"Hmmm—let me see," he said. "Yes, here it is . . . Spencer, Manor House . . . no, this is a report of a horse stolen, then recovered. That's all, Mrs. Wheeler. There's nothing else under Spencer. Try *The Sleepyside Sun*. The editor may remember something about it. He's owned the newspaper for thirty years."

Mrs. Wheeler thanked the sergeant and hung up the receiver.

"Are you going to call the *Sun?*" Trixie asked. "Here's the number," she said, "Sleepyside nine-six-eight-0."

Mrs. Wheeler dialed. Again the girls listened. The editor never had heard a report of any jewels missing.

"It sounds like a good feature story for the newspaper, however," he said. "Do you mind if I send a photographer and a reporter out to see the jewel box? Maybe we could get a picture of the Bob-White club members."

"I'll have to ask the girls about it first," Mrs. Wheeler told him. "I'll turn the receiver over to Trixie Belden. She's co-president of the club."

Trixie held a quick conference with the other girls.

"It'll be good publicity for the antique show," she whispered. "Let's tell him he may go ahead, shall we?"

The girls gave quick consent, and Trixie ended the conversation.

"Well, now, what shall we do with the musical jewel box?" Trixie asked.

"After the story is printed in the newspaper," Mrs. Wheeler said, "someone may claim it, though how it got in *our* attic I'll never know."

"And if someone doesn't claim it?" Trixie asked.

"I should think it would belong to the Bob-Whites," Mrs. Wheeler said, smiling. "Remember, I said you might have anything you found in that room in the attic. Let's just wait and see what happens. Yes, what is it, Celia?"

"A woman who says she is Mrs. Spencer wants to speak to you on the telephone," the maid said.

"Jeepers, what now?" Trixie asked.

"Come with me and I'll let you listen," Mrs. Wheeler said.

"I've been trying to call you for half an hour," Mrs. Spencer said, "but the line has been busy. Did the girls possibly find that jewel box in an old doll trunk?"

"Yes! Yes!" Trixie shouted excitedly into the receiver.

"That was Trixie Belden," Mrs. Wheeler explained. "The girls were so excited when they knew it was you calling that I'm letting them listen. Yes, they did find the jewel box in a doll's trunk. Why?"

"You'll never believe it," Mrs. Spencer said. "It's the strangest thing. One of my daughters is visiting me. She lives in Canada now. When I told her about my telephone conversation with you, she remembered something that happened when she and my other daughter were little girls."

"Why doesn't she go ahead and tell it?" Trixie said in a loud whisper.

Mrs. Spencer laughed. "Tell her I'm trying to tell the story," she said. "You know Mr. and Mrs. Frayne used to live in Ten Acres, near us. They didn't have any children and often invited my little girls to come over to their house to play. Margaret, my older daughter, who is here with me now, said Mrs. Frayne used to let them play with the musical jewel box.

"One day, when Mrs. Frayne was packing to go to Europe with Mr. Frayne, the girls were there. As usual, Mrs. Frayne gave them the musical jewel box to play with. When I sent for them to come home, they brought it with them. I hate to tell you the rest. . . ."

"Go on! Go on!" Trixie begged.

"Margaret says she is sure they had no idea of the value of the box—they were only about ten and eight years old at the time. Well, Mrs. Frayne went to Europe and the girls forgot to return the box. They were afraid I'd scold them if I found it in their room, so they decided to hide it in the attic. They had been using that old alphabet for some time to write notes to one another. That is why they put the message on the key tag. I guess all little girls like mysteries.

"That's the story. I don't believe Mrs. Frayne ever

mentioned the jewel box; certainly not in connection with my daughters. It's all very strange."

"Then, Mother," Honey said, when the conversation ended, "if the jewel box and rings belonged to Mrs. Frayne, they belong to Jim now, don't they?"

"I suppose they do," Mrs. Wheeler agreed, "since his uncle, James Frayne, left all the Frayne property to Jim."

"Whoops! Let's go and tell Jim!" Trixie shouted.

Dramatically Trixie told the story to the boys, as Honey exhibited the box. "What do you think of that?" she demanded when she had finished.

Brian and Mart stopped their work on the oil heater and exclaimed over the jewel box. Jim was strangely silent.

Alarmed, Trixie questioned him. "Why don't you say something, Jim? The jewel box and rings belong to you, now, of course. What's the matter?"

"It's just something my mother told me a long time ago," Jim said. "And because for once Jonesy, my step-father, was blamed for something he didn't do."

"You mean someone thought *he* stole the music box?" Trixie asked.

"Yes," Jim said. "My mother thought he did, too. My

Aunt Nell and Uncle Jim Frayne never liked him. They loved my mother, and they couldn't understand why she ever married Jonesy. Nobody could."

"What about the jewel box?" Trixie urged him. "What did you know about *it?*"

"I'm trying to tell you, Trixie," Jim said sadly. "My mother told me that when Aunt Nell came back from Europe she couldn't find the box anyplace, or the rings. She didn't mind the loss of the rings so very much, but Uncle Jim had given her the jewel box one time when they were in Paris. She loved it more than anything she owned. Jonesy used to ask my aunt and uncle for money, and, when my mother wouldn't let them give him any more, I guess Aunt Nell thought he stole the jewel box. When my mother accused him of it he denied it."

"That time he was right, wasn't he?" Trixie asked.

"Yes," Jim agreed. "I'd like to be able to tell him it's been found."

Trixie and Honey, who, when Ten Acres burned, had seen how cruel Jonesy could be, didn't waste much pity on him now. "Will you let us exhibit the jewel box at the show?" Trixie asked.

"Yes, of course," Jim answered. "The Bob-Whites can sell it and the rings, too, and add the money to the Fund."

"I'll bet your mother will buy it, Honey," Trixie said. "She thinks it's just beautiful," she added to Jim.

"Then she shall have it," Jim said at once. "I know Aunt Nell would have liked that. Mother's been so wonderful since she and Dad adopted me. The club can sell the rings. We'll just exhibit the jewel box."

The next day *The Sleepyside Sun* had a long story about the treasure found in the Manor House attic. The Bob-Whites spread the newspaper on the table in the school cafeteria. Nothing was said, of course, about the part Jim's stepfather played in the drama. There was a picture of Jim, however, of the jewel box, of all the Bob-Whites and their clubhouse, and a picture of Ten Acres before it burned.

"You made a lot of fuss about that jewel box," Mart said, "and you overlooked the keenest part of Trixie's discovery."

"What was that?" Trixie asked, all ears.

"The acrobatic alphabet, of course," Mart said. "We can use it for a secret code. If anyone gets into trouble, he sends a message in code, and we fly to the rescue!"

"You're right, Mart!" Trixie said. "Why didn't I think of using it for a club code? I'll go back and hunt it up again in that old magazine tonight."

"I *did* copy it from the magazine," Honey said. "I

have it here in my notebook. I'll make copies for all the Bob-Whites. We'll all have to learn it."

"We'll have to concentrate on learning the letters SOS at least," Mart said. "I'm afraid there are brains in this gathering incapable of assimilating the alphabet in its entirety."

"Skip it, Mart," Brian told his brother. "Don't forget that Trixie found the alphabet, that Trixie translated the message on the key tag, and that Trixie discovered the musical jewel box." He spread a paper napkin on the table, looked in Honey's notebook, and copied the three letters of the code.

"Maybe," he said, "if we all try hard enough we can get it through our heads that this means SOS and is a frantic call for help. And now let's get going to our classes."

Chapter 7
Thieves!

Every night after school the Bob-Whites worked. Jim and Brian polished the swords till they shone.

Then they gilded the frame of the old mirror. It was about forty-two inches square, and they had found an old gilt iron base to hold it. Refinished, it was beautiful.

Trixie washed and polished the two brown cooky jars. Inside one of them she found a pair of captain's epaulets from the Civil War. Since Honey's mother had no idea to whom they may have belonged, she told Honey the B.W.G.'s could keep them to sell at the show.

Diana, Trixie, and Honey helped Mart sand the two gate-leg tables.

Wednesday, at school, a bulletin announced a special teachers' meeting to be held at White Plains. This meant that the schools would not be open Thursday or Friday.

After they had left the clubhouse on Wednesday evening Trixie remembered that she had left her math notebook there. Brian had promised to help her finish her assignment that night, so the weekend would be free for club work.

"I'll go back and get the notebook," she said, "then I'll catch up with you."

All the Bob-Whites carried flashlights, because the path to the clubhouse led through the woods. Trixie threw the light ahead of her as she neared the clearing where the clubhouse stood. Snow covered the ground and her footsteps were silent.

A rabbit darted across her path. Startled, Trixie dropped her flashlight, and in the arc of light it made as it fell, two dark figures loomed. They were leaving the clubhouse area and climbing into a waiting car. With a growl from the exhaust, the car was off down the byway to Glen Road.

Terrified, Trixie gave the quick emergency call of the club, a double whistle, "Bob—Bob-White! Bob-White!"

Jim, Brian, and Mart came running. When she could get her breath Trixie told them what had happened.

"You're seeing things again," Mart said. "We only left here a second ago. Where were they then?"

"It wasn't a second. It was more than five minutes, and, anyway, Martin Belden, I know what I saw."

Brian had gone ahead to see if he could discover anything. He ran his flashlight around the door, then under the window.

"Someone was here," he said. "There are footprints, two sets of them. What on earth would anyone want to be snooping around here for? They must have kept watch on us and waited for us to go. Let's get Regan and come back. Mart, you take Trixie home."

"Nobody is going to take me home, Brian Belden," Trixie said. "I'm going right along with you. Why do we have to get Regan? We're not sissies. Let's go on through the woods down to Glen Road. Where are Diana and Honey?"

"They were so far ahead they didn't hear you whistle," Brian said. "They're probably at home by now. All right, Trixie, if you say you're going with us, you will. Some girls just never seem to know their place."

"And some boys think they know everything," Trixie said and strode off through the woods, the boys close after her.

There was definite evidence that someone had gone over the path recently. Their steps were fresh in the banked snow. The boys followed the path till it opened onto Glen Road. Then, dejected, they turned back home.

"That's a warning for us," Trixie said. "Someone

has read in the *Sun* about the jewel box and the antiques we have in the clubhouse. We'll have to guard them night and day."

"You know we can't do that," Jim said.

"We *can,* with a burglar alarm," Trixie said. "One that would sound in Regan's quarters, maybe."

"Say, I'll ask him about it—right away!" Jim said. "See you tomorrow."

"Wait a minute, Jim," Trixie said. "We'd better not say anything about what happened tonight except maybe to Regan. Moms might not want us to work at the club at night if she thought anyone might try to break in. We can keep a sharp lookout ourselves."

When they got back to Crabapple Farm the house was nearly dark. The family had gone to bed. "We don't have to answer any questions tonight," Trixie said, relieved.

The next morning after breakfast Mrs. Belden said, "Trixie, I have a book Mrs. Vanderpoel wants. It's about herbs, and she's going to try to grow some indoors this winter. Will you please take the book over to her? Take Bobby with you on his sled, please."

"Yes, Trixie, take me, I want a ride!" Bobby cried and went to get his coat and cap.

"All right, Moms," Trixie said, "but I thought it would be a good chance today to go out and try to locate some more furniture for the boys to repair, and maybe list some of the antiques we want to borrow to exhibit at our show."

"It is possible that Mrs. Vanderpoel may let you exhibit some of her antiques," Mrs. Belden said. "Don't you remember? Her house is full of them. She's lived in that one place for ages. Her parents, and their parents, too, lived there before her."

"I don't know why I didn't think of her," Trixie said. "Hurry, Bobby, let's go."

Mrs. Vanderpoel's home was of yellow brick. The bricks were small handmade ones, brought over from Holland by early Dutch settlers. The house was surrounded by trees, on a wandering road that led from Glen Road back about a mile through the woods, to the fringe of the game preserve Mr. Wheeler had recently bought.

"Giddyap, Trixie!" Bobby called. He imagined she was his trusty black horse carrying his sled over the snow. Trixie galloped on at his bidding, and, when rosy-cheeked old Mrs. Vanderpoel opened her back door to her knock, Trixie was too breathless to speak for a moment.

"Come in, children," Mrs. Vanderpoel said. "There are some oatmeal cookies—I've just finished baking. Sit down here beside Brom, Bobby, and I'll give you a glass of milk. There, there, Brom, these are the Belden children from Crabapple Farm."

An old man sat at the table, his face almost hidden in a bush of whiskers.

"Are you Rip van Winkle?" Bobby asked, as he scrambled into a chair and filled his mouth with a big cooky.

The old man laughed till he shook. "No, sir, Bobby, I'm not," he said. "I'm not Ichabod Crane either," he added, in a firmer voice. Trixie and Mrs. Vanderpoel had gone into another room. Brom was shy, but not with little boys.

"I know you're not Ichabod Crane," Bobby said. "He was as thin as a skeleton and you're—"

"I'm certainly not skinny," the old man said. "My name is Brom—just Brom. There's another name, too, but it's a long Dutch name and you wouldn't remember it."

"It's Vanderheidenbeck," Mrs. Vanderpoel said to Trixie in a whisper. "He'd close up like a clam if he knew we were listening. Stay right here with me behind the door, Trixie. When Brom talks it is worth listening."

"I couldn't get skinny," Brom went on, "the way Mrs. Vanderpoel feeds me. When I get hungry I just rap at her door. How'd you find out about Rip van Winkle, Bobby?"

" 'Cause Sleepyside isn't very far from Sleepy Hollow," Bobby said. "The story's in all the books."

"Is that so?" old Brom wondered. "Is that so? I can tell you stories you'll never find in any books, Bobby, and they're all true. The Hudson River Valley and the Catskill Mountains are full of witches and ghosts and goblins—it just takes a certain kind of eyes to be able to see them."

"Do you have that kind of eyes?" Bobby asked.

"I do," old Brom answered. "Listen—you've never heard of No-mah-ka-ta, the witch who lives on top of the highest mountains in the Catskills, have you?"

"No, sir," said Bobby. "Is she a *real* witch?"

"Yes, indeed," Brom said. "In the morning she lets the day out of the dark cave where it's been all night. At night No-mah-ka-ta puts the day back in the cave and everything is black as night."

"An' the owls come out," Bobby said.

"That they do, Bobby," old Brom said. "But when No-mah-ka-ta wants light in the sky at night she hangs out a new moon."

"What does she do with the old ones?" Bobby asked, his eyes as big as saucers.

"She cuts them up into stars," Brom said.

"She must be a good witch," Bobby said.

"No," Brom said thoughtfully, "I've seen her when she was good and mad."

"You really *saw* the witch?" Bobby asked.

"That's right," Brom said. "I've seen her right there on top of her mountain spinning clouds and flinging them to the four winds. Of course, some people would say it was just the mist I saw, blown by the wind."

"I like the wind," Bobby said.

"Yes," Brom said, "the soft west wind. But No-mah-ka-ta spins wild winds, too, when she is cross—black winds that bring rain, rain that floods the earth and sweeps away houses."

"Brom will go on like that for an hour," Mrs. Vanderpoel said, "as long as there is a little child to tell his stories to. What are you looking at, child?"

"Your wonderful, wonderful old furniture," Trixie said as Mrs. Vanderpoel led her into the big family room. "That little melodeon—may I touch it?"

"You sit right down and play on it, Trixie," said Mrs. Vanderpoel, turning the stool to the right height. "It has a pretty tone, hasn't it? Land, you've seen it a

94

dozen times, and the rest of the furniture, too."

"It's different now, though," Trixie said. "I've always thought it was beautiful, but now . . ."

She told Mrs. Vanderpoel about the antique show they were planning. She told of the reason for the show, of the need for money for little children far across the oceans.

She didn't have enough courage to ask Mrs. Vanderpoel if they could exhibit some of her heirlooms. She did not need to ask. Mrs. Vanderpoel offered them to the Bob-Whites.

"You say you only want to borrow them overnight and for one day?" she asked.

"That's all," Trixie told her. "I'll come after them with Tom and Regan myself and watch to see that there isn't a scratch on them."

"Mercy, I don't worry about that," Mrs. Vanderpoel said. "Children have played around my furniture for several generations. They've never done any harm that a little rubbing with cabinet-maker's wax won't cure. Just tell me what you want for the show and I'll have it ready and shined. I'm going to give you this small carved oak lap desk," she said. "It belonged to my father. I'd like to think the money for it would be used to help children."

"That's wonderful!" Trixie exclaimed. "Why, our

tickets won't go begging when people hear about these beautiful things!"

"There are some pieces in the lean-to kitchen, too," Mrs. Vanderpoel went on. "I've been wondering what to do with them. They need a touch here and there to repair them, and from what you tell me Brian and Mart and Jim can do that. Brom would do it if he could, but he's forgetful."

"I've never seen him before," Trixie said. "I've heard of him, though, but I didn't think he was real. People say he's another Rip van Winkle."

"He lives in a small cottage on the property that used to belong to his family, a very old Dutch family, older than my own. The wooded land is part of Mr. Wheeler's game preserve now. He is so proud he never asks for anything. Sometimes, though, when he gets hungry, he comes to my door. I am proud to be able to offer him my hospitality."

As she finished talking they walked back into the kitchen. Bobby was sitting on Brom's knee. The old man's arm was tight around him. Bobby seemed to be his dear new-found friend.

"Mr. Brom knows the wonderfulest stories," Bobby explained, "about witches an'—well, one witch anyway. Mr. Brom is goin' to come and see me some day."

"Then you really *are* his friend, Bobby," Mrs. Vanderpoel said.

"Please do come to see us," Trixie said. "We'd all love to have you come, Mr. Brom." Through the window Trixie could see the snow. "It's snowing hard, Mrs. Vanderpoel," she said. "I think Bobby and I had better start home. Do you think we could take the lap desk on the sled? I want Mart to see it, and the rest of the Bob-Whites. Maybe I should wait till later."

"No, go right ahead and take it, Trixie. Brom, do you think you could carry it out to the sled for Trixie?"

The old man jumped up quickly. "I'll call that young man who's shoveling the walk to help you settle it on the sled," Mrs. Vanderpoel said to Brom. "Young man, come here, please!" she said as she opened the door.

"Now, Trixie, come and I'll show you the things in the lean-to shed—just a once-over look so you'll know what to tell the boys," Mrs. Vanderpoel said.

"You be careful of that desk now," Bobby warned the big boy as he lowered Mrs. Vanderpoel's gift onto Bobby's lap. "It's a anteek for the Bob-Whites to sell at their show."

"For how much?" the big boy asked.

"About a hunnerd dollars I guess," Bobby boasted.

"An' that's not all. There's lots of other things Mrs. Vanderpoel's goin' to let the Bob-Whites take for their show next month. They're worth zillions of dollars."

Old Brom bent down and rubbed his hand over the oak desk. "It's pretty," he said.

"Yeah," the big boy said, thoughtfully. "Yeah, it is, now, ain't it?" He propped the snow shovel against a tree and ran off across the yard and into the woods.

It was snowing heavily, but Trixie started off briskly on the mile journey home. It was drifting on the wood path, but she knew the going would be better when she reached Glen Road.

"Sing me a song, Trixie," Bobby said. "This desk is sorta heavy."

"Pull it up farther on your lap, Bobby," Trixie said, "over your knees."

Then she sang at the top of her voice, "Over the river and through the woods . . ." Bobby joined in the chorus. It was silent and near dark in the big woods, and their voices echoed back.

"That's enough of that singing!" a voice called out to them, and Trixie stopped, frozen in fright. Three men came through the undergrowth and stopped in her path. Their faces were covered with stocking tops drawn tight to conceal their features.

Bobby thought it was great fun. "Robbers!" he cried. "I'll get you!" He made a snowball to throw at them.

"Cut it out, kid!" one of the men said. "We ain't playin'. We mean business."

As he spoke the other two seized the sled, upset desk and Bobby, then dragged the sled and desk off through the woods.

"I couldn't hold on to it, Trixie," Bobby cried, tears mixing with the snow that covered his face. "They stealed your desk! Honest, I couldn't hold on to it."

"Never mind, honey," Trixie said. She was trembling so she could hardly speak, but her first thought was of her young brother. "Let Trixie brush you off, lamb," she said. "Don't cry. Spider will catch those bad men. There now, I'll just put you down on the path. You'll have to walk now, Bobby, and we've still a long way to go."

Trixie was angry, bitterly angry at the three thieves who had robbed them. "Spider will get them," she promised Bobby.

"I'm cold, Trixie," the little boy said. "An' it's dark a'most. Are we losted?"

"No, honey. Here, take my hand. Left foot! Right foot! Left foot! Right foot! Marching! Marching!"

Bobby kept up sturdily for a while, then his steps slowed. "I—just—can't—walk—any more," he said and he sat down in the snow.

"Try just a little harder, Bobby," Trixie urged. "See, through the trees, that's Glen Road ahead."

"I can't see anything, Trixie. I'll just sit here and rest," Bobby said and settled down into the deep snow.

"No, Bobby, we have to hurry home. Those men may still be around the woods. I'll carry you." Trixie was so worried she hardly noticed his weight. She was afraid he would be sick, he was so tired and chilled.

Trixie was tired, too; very, very tired when she finally set Bobby down on the path that led to Glen Road.

There, to her great relief, she saw Brian and Mart coming down the road. Mrs. Belden, concerned with the lateness and approaching dark, had sent the boys to meet them.

At home Bobby was given a warm, comforting bath and put to bed. Trixie had a hard time calming down enough to tell her story.

With great difficulty she, Mart, and Brian kept their father from going off to the police in Sleepyside.

"Don't you see," Trixie said, "if we make a big fuss about the oak desk, a lot of other people may find out about the things in Mrs. Vanderpoel's house and break in . . . and they may break in the clubhouse."

"She's right, Dad," Brian insisted. "Spider will help us find out who stole the desk. He probably knows about the gang already. . . ."

"See that you get in touch with Spider tomorrow, then," Mr. Belden said. "I'll check with him when I see him."

"Oh, Daddy, please don't do that," Trixie begged. "Let us Bob-Whites handle it with him, won't you? After all, it's *our* show."

"And you want to be self-sufficient," Mr. Belden said. "I'm always telling your mother to let you manage your own affairs. I guess I'd better take some of my own advice."

It was left that way.

The next morning Bobby had a bad cold. For days his temperature ran high and the doctor said Bobby had pneumonia. He was a very sick boy, so sick that it drove every thought of anything else out of the minds of the Belden family.

Chapter 8
Foreign Intrigue

With good medicine and his mother's careful nursing, Bobby grew better. While he had been critically ill it had been hard for the Bob-Whites to turn their attention to their work.

Trixie had, however, gone with the Wheelers' chauffeur, Tom, back to Mrs. Vanderpoel's to bring out the other furniture she said they could have—the furniture that needed to be repaired.

Trixie did not tell Mrs. Vanderpoel what had happened to the desk. She was ashamed to tell and, too, she hoped they would recover it soon. She would wait a little longer before saying anything about it.

"Did you see anything of that boy who was shoveling my walks when you were here last time?" Mrs. Vanderpoel asked.

"No," Trixie answered. "Why do you ask, Mrs. Vanderpoel?"

"It's the first time anyone ever worked for me and ran off without waiting to be paid," Mrs. Vanderpoel said. "I never saw him before he stopped and asked for work. Oh well, he'll stop and ask for his pay, too, I guess."

"I wonder," Trixie said to herself on the way home, "I wonder if that boy had anything to do with the desk. I just wonder."

In the clubhouse after school, they all worked hard getting ready for the show. The oil heater kept them cozy and warm, and the new electric lights made it possible to work after dark. Also, Regan had installed an alarm system attached to a wire leading to his apartment over the stable at Manor House. It hadn't buzzed once, and there had been no disturbance since the night the two men were trying to look into the clubhouse.

"It must have been the same ones who stole the lap desk," Honey said. "Do you think we'll ever be able to find out any more about that or get the desk back?"

"Not unless we try harder than we've been trying," Trixie said and told them what Mrs. Vanderpoel had told her about the boy who ran off without being paid.

"He might have been one of them," Jim said thoughtfully. "He was, of course. Brian and I have tried to locate Spider half a dozen times to ask him about it. We haven't been able to find him."

"That seems strange," Trixie said, worried. "It's almost as though he's trying to keep out of our way."

"Why would he want to do that?" Diana asked.

"He's been acting so queer lately," Trixie said.

The next day, instead of meeting the others in the school cafeteria for lunch, Trixie started out to try to find Spider. Until they could discover who the thieves were, everything they had in the clubhouse was in danger.

Trixie's intuition led her directly to where Spider was having a break for lunch, to Wimpy's Diner where they had seen him the night of the school board meeting. Trixie climbed up on a stool next to Spider and nudged his arm.

"Hello, there," Spider said. "How's the head of the Intelligence Department today?"

"Spider," Trixie said seriously, ignoring his sarcasm, "we're having trouble, the Bob-Whites are. Someone was looking into the clubhouse one night. We had been having a meeting. They must have waited till they saw us leave, then tried to get in one of the windows."

"How did you know?" Spider asked.

"I went back suddenly and saw them leaving," Trixie told him.

"Did you recognize any of them?" Spider asked anxiously.

"No, but that isn't all." She told him about the masked men who dumped Bobby into the snow and stole the desk.

"What do you want me to do about it?" Spider asked. "I think you might as well forget it."

Trixie, amazed at his attitude, insisted, "We *can't* forget it, Spider. They'll keep on doing things like that."

"It was probably some kids playing a trick on you and now they're afraid to return it. We find that all the time," Spider said. "The desk will turn up one of these days in some out-of-the-way corner where they've hidden it."

"Spider Webster!" Trixie said. "Those men who took the desk had masks on. They were real crooks."

Spider waved his hand nervously. "Forget it, Trixie. There are half a hundred things more important that are bothering the police."

"Well, they're going to get a chance to bother once more," Trixie said vehemently. "I don't understand you, Spider. I'm going to march myself right down to the police station and report it now."

"Don't do it!" Spider warned.

Trixie hesitated, her hand on the doorknob. "What do you mean?"

"I mean just this," Spider said, his face reddening, "that you'll get your club into more trouble than Mr. Stratton caused. Who do you suppose complained to him and to the board about secret societies in the first place?"

"The police?" asked Trixie.

"Figure it out yourself," said Spider. "Since that business came up with the school board there hasn't been any more vandalism at the school, has there?"

"No," Trixie admitted. "I'd give a good deal to know who did that damage at the school. What do you mean when you say the vandalism stopped after the talks we had with Mr. Stratton?"

"I mean just this: Maybe it *was* an inside job at the school. Maybe some kid did it for spite because he'd been shut out of the clubs."

"He wouldn't *steal* for that reason," Trixie said.

"How do you know what a kid would do if he didn't have the right guidance at home?" Spider asked. "You and the Wheeler and Lynch kids don't know what it is to be up against trouble. You've always had it easy."

"Why, Spider Webster, we work hard, every one of us."

"Yeah, but your folks make it easy for you. It wouldn't hurt any of you to be a little bit nicer to some of the other kids in school who don't have it so good." Spider's face was serious.

Trixie didn't answer for a little while. Then she said thoughtfully, "Maybe we do stick together too much. I guess it's just because we've been working so hard. I never thought about it before, Spider. Maybe you're right."

"You just bet I'm right," Spider said. "You kids always high-hat Tad, for instance. I know he's not perfect, but he's not bad either. All that business about helping kids on the other side of the world—try to do something for some kids nearer home."

"Why, Spider," Trixie said sadly, "we *have* been pretty selfish, haven't we? Not a single one of the Bob-Whites ever wanted to be. I know that. I'm going to talk to them about what you've said. Thanks, Spider."

After school Trixie told the rest of the B.W.G.'s that Spider didn't think the mysterious visit to the clubhouse was very important.

"Don't worry too much about it," Mart said. "He'll come around to helping us. Remember when we were shut up in that red trailer, and had such a time convincing Spider we were really kidnaped?"

"I remember," Honey said. "You told us you had to bring out a tape recording of that man's voice to prove it to Spider. He's queer."

"I think he's worried about Tad," Diana said.

"You don't mean that he thinks Tad stole the desk?" Honey asked.

"No, he doesn't think that," Trixie said. "It's something a lot different, and I'm ashamed. I think you will all be, too, after I tell you!" So she told them of her conversation with Spider.

"He makes us sound like a bunch of snobs," Mart said. "And we're not. I'm downright jealous of Tad because he's in the Pony League and I'm not."

"Tell Tad so some time," Trixie said. "I think Spider is right, in a way. Maybe we *have* been thoughtless and didn't mean anything, but if you think about it as I have since I talked to Spider, you'll realize how much we keep to ourselves. It isn't only after school hours, but at school, too."

"Tad *is* a kind of goon," Diana insisted.

"Maybe he wouldn't be if we'd be a little more decent to him," Trixie said. "I, for one, am going to try."

"It won't hurt the rest of us to try, too," Jim said. "Right, gang?"

"Right!" they answered.

109

"I just hope Spider will help us find out a few things," Trixie continued, her point made. "There's some kind of a hook-up among those people who were looking into the clubhouse that night, the masked robbers who stole the desk, that boy who was shoveling snow, and even the schoolhouse vandals."

It was only a few days later when part of that theory was disproved.

The Bob-Whites were all at the clubhouse working: Honey and Diana were stuffing the cloth dolls, Mart was working on a chair, and Brian and Jim were looking over a group of framed pictures that had been given them. Trixie was sitting at a table surrounded by papers, arranging the route for Tom and Regan to follow to pick up the antiques to be exhibited.

"Someone's coming round the corner of the clubhouse," Honey announced.

A knock sounded at the door.

Brian answered it. A small Japanese man stood there, hat in hand, bowing. "Please, I like to talk to the boss girl," he said.

"We don't have any boss," Mart said, standing back of Brian. Then he added politely, "Won't you come in?"

"He probably means Trixie," Jim said, smiling. "If we have a boss, she's it."

"Miss Trixie, yes," said the Japanese man. "Cook at Wheeler house tell me Miss Trixie have sword, I think maybe old samurai sword."

Trixie looked a little shamefaced. She didn't realize she had such a reputation for being bossy. "Jim and Brian and Mart know about the swords," she said. "They polished them and oiled them. Would you like to see them?"

"Yes, please," the Japanese man said.

So Brian and Jim took the swords down from the closet wall where they had hung them. The Japanese man picked up the longer sword and held it lovingly, running his right thumb up and down the single cutting edge.

He took it over under the strongest light to examine the marking on the hilt. Then he picked up the dagger and examined it just as carefully.

"Very old samurai swords," he said. "Very old. Maybe belong to Satsuma clan. You sell them?"

"We hope to sell them when we have our antique show next month," Trixie said. "We couldn't sell them before that, could we, Jim?"

"Not without breaking our club agreement," Jim told her.

"You see, Mr.—"

"Oto Hakaito," he said and bowed. *He seems to be always bowing,* Trixie thought.

"You see, Mr. Hakaito," she explained, "we agreed among ourselves that we wouldn't sell anything from our collection *before* the show. Several people have wanted to buy certain articles, and we thought it would only be fair if everyone had the same chance the day of the show. Someone else asked about the swords."

"Yes, I know," the Japanese man said, bowing again. "My brother Kasyo and I would very much like to buy samurai swords."

Then Oto turned around to the B.W.G.'s, circled around them, and bowed again. "I have confession to make," he said. "Samurai swords very much loved by Japanese people. In Tokyo is big museum where are many swords. My brother and I like to buy these swords. Send them to museum in Tokyo. Make our father who live in that city very proud."

"What did you mean by 'confession'?" Mart asked. "There isn't anything wrong about wanting to buy the old swords."

"Confession is this," Oto Hakaito said sadly. "One night, the night Miss Honey's cook told us about the swords, we come here, my brother and I, to ask to see them. When we arrive there is no one here. So," he

continued, "we cannot wait. We flash light through windows to try to see swords. We very much disappointed no one home. You angry?"

"Of course we aren't angry," Trixie said, relieved. "I was scared that night, though. I saw you. I went back for my notebook just in time to see you get into your car and leave. We thought you were thieves."

"Hakaito brothers *not* thieves," Oto said quickly. "Good vegetable gardeners, not thieves. Why you not call to us? We come back."

"I was too scared," Trixie said. "I'm relieved now, to know who it was."

Oto Hakaito showed his white teeth in a broad smile. "Still cannot buy samurai swords?" he asked.

"No chance now," said Trixie and Jim together. Then Jim went on, "We will see, however, that you have the fairest kind of a chance at the show."

"I thank you very much," said Oto Hakaito, bowing deeply as he turned to leave.

"Well," Jim said, "that blows up your theory, Trixie, that the mysteries were related. I'm sure the Hakaito brothers had nothing to do with stealing the desk."

"Who are the Hakaito brothers?" Brian asked. "Does anyone know?"

"I think they have a truck garden on the other side

of Sleepyside," Honey answered. "And a produce shop in town. I'm pretty sure they are the ones who sell vegetables and fruits to our cook."

"That figures," said Mart. "That's how they found out about the swords. I hope they are able to buy them. They belong in Tokyo if the Japanese think that much of them."

"I think they do, too," Trixie said. "But why would Honey's family's cook talk to Japanese gardeners about swords?"

"It could come about in the most natural way," Mart answered. "Don't imagine a lot of foreign intrigue. You are inadequately equipped to cope with a problem of such magnitude."

Trixie snorted.

"Translated, Mart means you've enough to occupy your mind in this hemisphere," Jim said. "Keep out of Asia!"

"You all make me tired," Trixie said. "When something comes up, the rest of you just sit back and wonder and wish. *I* do something about it. Then you make fun of me. Why doesn't someone else get busy and find out where that desk is, and who upset a little boy and gave him pneumonia?"

"Phewwww! We've been trying," Mart said. "You

don't do all your sleuthing singlehanded, either."

"Sometimes I wish she did," Honey said. "I'm a sleuth against my will."

"The Reluctant Flatfoot," Mart called her. "Maybe Spider is right and the desk will turn up in some odd place."

Chapter 9
Lost in a Blizzard

"I'm afraid we can't work on the furniture at the club tonight," Honey told Trixie when they met in the corridor on their way to class. "Or try to solve any mysteries either."

"Why not?" Trixie asked. "We have to use every minute we can. Why can't we work?"

"Because Regan is pretty mad at us. He says we never help him exercise the horses any more," Honey said.

Trixie's face fell. "We can't afford to have Regan mad at us," she said. "He's one of the best friends anyone ever had."

"Miss Trask, too. She said she never sees us any more. She misses Bobby particularly." Honey was exasperated with Trixie at times. She wished her friend wouldn't try to solve every mystery all by herself. Honey wanted to be the kind of detective who sat in an office and directed other people. She had no liking for danger.

Trixie was just the opposite. The more involved a situation seemed to be, the better she liked it.

Adventure—even danger—beckoned to her and found her willing. The mysterious happenings that annoyed Honey and, in fact, the other members of the Bob-Whites of the Glen only excited Trixie. She would like to spend every moment with the club and its problems.

Trixie was scrupulous, though, about doing work that was expected of her. If Regan wanted the horses exercised, she would do it, no matter what she would rather do. Until Honey Wheeler's family had bought Manor House, Trixie had never had a chance to ride a horse, and she had longed for one. Now the Wheelers' five riding horses were at the disposal of Honey's and Jim's friends. Red-haired Regan lost his red-haired temper when the horses weren't exercised and everything wasn't shipshape around the stables.

"We'll tell the boys when we meet them at noon that we have to ride," Honey said. "Regan surely can use some help. He's had Tom, our chauffeur, riding. If there's anything Tom hates more than being away from the cars I don't know what it is."

"That's true," Trixie agreed. "And if there's anything Regan hates more than an automobile, it's another automobile. They're both super at the jobs they have."

"That's why my daddy doesn't want anything to happen that might make either of them want to leave,"

Honey said. "Why can't Bobby come over to our house and visit Miss Trask and Regan tonight after school? He used to be with them often before he was sick. Diana's little twin brothers Larry and Terry have been at our house several times. Regan is crazy about children. He was raised in an orphanage, and I guess that's the reason. Can't Bobby come over?"

"I'm afraid not. I thought you knew that Bobby hasn't been allowed to go out of the house yet. He hasn't quite recovered from his sickness after that desk was stolen. I wish Miss Trask and Regan would come to see him. You remember old Brom, the man with the whiskers who was at Mrs. Vanderpoel's house? I told you about him. He comes to see Bobby often. He just loves him. He doesn't have money to buy presents for Bobby, but the things he brings are wonderful. He made a willow whistle for Bobby that plays several notes."

"I'd love to see it," Honey said.

"He carved queer little witches and goblins for Bobby, too," Trixie said. "I think Brom really thinks the elves live in the mountains near here. I *know* Bobby believes it. You should hear some of the legends old Brom tells Bobby. If someone would put them in a book, I know the book would sell."

"Maybe some day we could collect them," Honey

suggested, "if Brom would tell them to us so we could write them down. That would be a good project for the B.W.G.'s, wouldn't it?"

"Not for me," Trixie said. "You know the kind of marks I get in English."

"The poems you wrote for your term paper were beautiful—the ones about the Navaho Indians. You wrote them after we came back from the ranch," Honey said. "You got an *A* on them."

"All I did was to repeat some of the ceremonial songs," Trixie said, "and maybe twist them around a bit. I can't write prose. Poems sing inside my head at times. It's when I try to put them down on paper that I fail. Jeepers, Honey, we're going to be late for class. The corridor is deserted. I didn't hear the bell, did you?"

"Not a sound," Honey said and they hurried into the English classroom.

At noon when Trixie told the boys that Regan was provoked at them for not helping exercise the horses, Jim said, "Honey must have seen Regan yesterday instead of today, or she must have misunderstood. Brian and Mart and I rode all the horses last evening. We took turns. I saw Tom this morning riding Susie, and Mother had Strawberry."

"That leaves Jupiter, Lady, and Starlight," Honey said.

"I'll ride Jupiter tonight," Brian said. He usually rode the chestnut gelding Starlight, but he longed to give Jupiter, Jim's big black gelding, a real workout.

"Not tonight, Brian," Jim said. "He hasn't had enough exercise lately and he'll be too hard to manage. I'll take him. I seem to have put the Indian sign on him. He's better with me than with anyone else. We'll all have to pay more attention to exercising the horses from now on."

"Let me ride Starlight," Mart begged. "You said I could, Brian."

Brian nodded his permission.

"I'll ride Lady," Honey said.

"Then Brian and I'll go home and help Moms," Trixie said. "It's hard to do everything. We just *have* to work every minute we can on the furniture. We just *have* to study, too, and to help at home. I don't know what Tad can find to make him jealous. We work harder than people do in the mines in Africa."

"I think you are confusing, in your usual befuddled manner, Africa with Siberia," Mart said smugly. "If you'd do a little reading now and then, instead of pursuing elusive individuals who practice infraction of the law, you'd—"

"I'd be as big a bore as you are, Mart Belden, with your big words that don't mean anything," Trixie, her face red, retorted.

"Don't argue, please," Diana said. "Remember, we have to work together."

"All right, little dove of peace," Mart said. He really liked Diana. She had a way of smoothing his feathers when they bristled.

Though Mart and Trixie seemed usually to be at swords' points, if anyone said a word against either one of them, the other would spring to his defense immediately. It was just that they were too near one another in age. Because Mart was eleven months older, and a boy, and for that reason seemed to enjoy a few extra privileges, Trixie continuously tried to get even with him.

When the school bus stopped at Manor House that afternoon, Mart got off with Honey, Jim, and Diana. Diana usually cut across the upper part of the Wheeler estate to get to her own home. Trixie and Brian went on to Crabapple Farm.

Jim's black and white springer spaniel, Patch, ran out barking and waving his tail like a semaphore. Regan, leading Jupiter, called to Jim, "Tell him to be quiet! He's making Jupiter nervous, but he won't mind me."

"You know I've trained him to mind only me," Jim said. "Heel, Patch!" The little dog dropped behind Jim and froze into immediate obedience. It was such a beautiful performance that everyone applauded, even the bus driver.

Jim stooped to pull the little dog's ears affectionately.

"We're sorry about not exercising the horses," Trixie called from the bus. "It's just that we've been so busy working on the antique show."

"I know that," Regan said, "but the horses don't. You'll have to do better, Trixie, or we'll have a bunch of wild horses on our hands and nothing to ride in the spring."

The bus driver stepped on the accelerator. "We'll do better," Trixie called through the window. "See if we don't."

The bus went on down the valley to Crabapple Farm.

"I'm surely glad you came home to help," Mrs. Belden said. "This has been a day when everything seemed to go wrong. I haven't had a minute to feed the chickens, and Bobby has been so cross."

"I wasn't cross," Bobby called from the couch in the den. "I just wanted to get up and play with Reddy, and Moms never letted me."

"That's another thing," Mrs. Belden said. "I haven't seen Reddy since morning. He always keeps Bobby amused. He's never stayed away from him this long before. Open a can of his food and go out and call him, please, Brian."

Brian called, "Reddy! Here, Reddy! Come, Reddy!"

But no Reddy came bounding out of the woods as he usually did at the first sound of his name.

"He didn't come when I called, Moms," Brian said and put the can of dog food on the table in the kitchen.

"It's strange," Mrs. Belden said. "He probably chased a rabbit far into the heart of the game preserve. The Wheelers' gamekeeper, Mr. Maypenny, won't like that at all."

"Mr. Maypenny is away," Trixie said.

"I want my dog," Bobby wailed. "My dog is losted. Please find my dog."

"He isn't lost, lamb," Trixie said. "He'll be home soon."

Trixie wasn't sure of what she was saying. She could see that her mother was concerned, too, and that Brian was worried. The whole family loved the playful Irish setter.

"He is too losted. I'll go and hunt for him myself," Bobby insisted.

"I'm sure he'll be home soon," his mother assured him. "Trixie will read to you, Bobby."

"Don't want another old story. I only like the ones Brom tells me. Where's Brom? Is he losted, too? He didn't come to see me for two years!" Bobby was tired of being kept in the house all the time, and he was unreasonable.

"Look out the window, lamb," Trixie said. "That's right, you may get up and go to the window. See who's there!"

"It's Jim!" Bobby cried. "He's riding Jupiter! Moms, may I go out and see Jupiter and Jim?"

"No, you may not, Bobby. Why do you continue to ask me if you may go out-of-doors when the doctor said you couldn't until the weather grows warmer?" Mrs. Belden was tired or she would never have lost patience with any of her children, and least of all with Bobby.

Bobby did not notice, however. He put his face up against the window. Jim turned Jupiter so the big horse's black nose was pressed against Bobby's, with just the glass between.

"Come in, Jim, and talk to me," Bobby insisted. "Bring Jupiter in to see me!"

Jim laughed. "I can't do that, Bobby," he called, "but

I'll put Jupiter out in the barn. Then I'll come in for a while."

"Give Jupiter some oats to eat!" Bobby shouted. "Call Reddy, too, please. I'm afraid Reddy is really losted, Moms," he said as he lay down again on the couch in the study. "Jim will go and find him for me."

"What's this about Reddy?" Jim asked when he came in through the kitchen.

"I don't know," Trixie answered. "He doesn't come when we call him. It's never happened before, especially if he hasn't been fed all day. Did you call him?"

"As loud as I could call when I came out of the barn," Jim said. "Don't you think someone should go and hunt for him?"

"I thought so, but Moms is worried. She doesn't want us to go far from the farm. She thinks a blizzard is coming. Bobby is fretting so, though."

Trixie turned to her mother, "Moms, won't you please let us go? Brian and I know our way through all the woods around here. We've been in blizzards before. Please!"

"If you don't let Trixie go and find my dog I'll get sick again," Bobby called from the study.

"I'll go with you to look for Reddy," Jim said. "I can leave Jupiter in the barn here till I come back. Don't you

think it would be all right if the three of us were together, Mrs. Belden?"

Trixie looked expectantly at her mother.

"I just don't know what to say," Mrs. Belden replied.
"If your father were only here," she added, "but he is in
New York on business. He won't be back till tomorrow."

"Reddy'll just die if they wait till tomorrow," Bobby
cried. "Plll . . . eease let Trixie go and find my dog."

"What's all the fuss about, Moms?" Brian asked.
"You're not usually so reluctant to let us do anything."

"I'm nervous," Mrs. Belden said. "It sounds foolish,
but I'm afraid something will happen."

"What kind of something?" Trixie asked. "You're
imagining things."

"Maybe I am," her mother agreed. "Why don't you
let the boys go by themselves?"

"Trixie is the one who will find my dog," Bobby
cried. "I want Trixie to go."

"Very well," Mrs. Belden said. "But if it starts to
snow hard you come back, will you?"

"If we think the storm is turning into a blizzard, we
will," Trixie answered, exultant. She loved to be out in a
storm. She loved any kind of adventure, and almost any
kind of hazard. In a few minutes she was back with her
big car coat, and with a woolen scarf to tie over her head.

"Jim, you take this heavy sweater," Mrs. D⸺ said. "You're just dressed for riding. Do you have your flashlights? Remember, Trixie, this is *no* adventure. You're going to find Reddy, and when you find him, you come right straight back home!"

"Brian and I will try to curb her curiosity," Jim said and winked at Trixie as the three of them left.

The thing Jim liked best about Trixie was her spirit of adventure, her readiness to go anywhere any time and not hold back, afraid, as so many girls did.

Lately Jim had been noticing, too, that Trixie was a pretty girl. Just now his eyes brightened in approval at the picture she made in her great red car coat and scarlet scarf. Her eyes were as clear blue as a summer sky, and her cheeks flushed pink with excitement.

Trixie looped a leash over her arm. It was an indignity Reddy seldom suffered. He hated a leash, but he must be taught that he could not run away.

They set off briskly through the woods. From time to time they stopped to call the setter. "Reddy! Here, Reddy! Come, boy!"

There was no response.

"Maybe someone picked him up," Jim said. "Someone in a car over on Glen Road."

"It would take a squad of mounted police to get

Reddy into a strange car," Trixie said. "I'm worried."

"Now don't go feminine on us," Brian warned.

"Brian Belden, you're worried yourself!" Trixie said.

"Both of you had *better* be a little worried," Jim said, pushing his way through the path. "Do you see how the wind has changed? Where is the sun?"

"It's getting late in the day," Trixie said. "It must be past four o'clock. No, Jim, you're right! Listen to that wind!"

"It's about ten degrees colder, too," Brian said, beating his chest to keep the blood circulating. "Where *is* that dog? Here, Reddy! Here, Reddy!"

"How do you know he even came this way?" Jim asked.

"He always *has* followed this path, or gone into the woods on this part of the preserve," Trixie answered. "He's here in the forest somewhere."

"But where?" Brian asked. "I don't like the way that wind is acting."

"Now who's scared?" Trixie asked.

"Maybe *you* should go back, Trixie," Jim suggested.

"I'll never do that," Trixie answered. "I'll go back when both of you go back, and not before. I don't think I'd go back even then. Just think of listening to Bobby cry all night long if we don't find Reddy. No, I'm going right on."

"You'll have to do the explaining to Moms," Brian said, "if we get lost. I hope *you* know where we are. I don't. Do you, Jim?"

"I . . . don't . . . think . . . so," Jim said slowly. "Trixie, let's make one last attempt to call Reddy. Then we must turn back. Okay?"

"Yes, Jim," Trixie said meekly. "But I don't want to give up."

Brian and Jim beat back the snow-covered bushes on each side of the path and called, "Here, Reddy!"

There was no answering bark, only silence.

"Here, Reddy!" Trixie called softly, coaxingly. "Here, Reddy boy! Come, Reddy!"

A half moan, half bark answered her.

"He's near here!" she called to the boys. "Right around here someplace. Where are you, Reddy? I'm coming!"

The whimper and bark grew a little louder. They turned in its direction. The snow was coming down in a thick heavy cloud. Even beneath the trees the fall was so dense they could see only a little way ahead of them in the fast-gathering dusk.

"Reddy?" Trixie kept calling. "Reddy?" The answering

whine was so near she almost stumbled over the big red dog lying on the ground.

"What is it, Reddy?" Trixie asked, down on her knees at his side. "Good Reddy, good dog, are you hurt?" Reddy licked her hand in welcome.

"He's caught in a trap," Brian said, kneeling on the dog's other side. "It must be his leg—yes, there it is. Quiet, fella, I'll try not to hurt you. His foot is caught— just the tip. Thank goodness it isn't any worse." Brian released the trap.

"Good Reddy!" Trixie said, hugging their pet. "Is his foot broken, Brian?"

"No, but it must hurt pretty bad. There, there, Reddy boy!" Brian lifted the big dog into his arms.

"Who'd be so cruel as to set a trap around here?" Trixie asked. "I hope you'll ask your father to have Mr. Maypenny look into it right away, Jim."

"It's an old fox trap, all rusted," Jim announced. "There's a bounty on fox pelts now. Someone must have found this old trap someplace and set it to try to make some money. Poor Reddy!"

"It could have been worse," Brian said. "I know you don't think so, boy," he said, as Reddy snuggled his damp nose against Brian's neck.

"I'd say Reddy's in better shape than we are right

now," Jim said. "I haven't the slightest idea where we are. I just know there's the granddaddy of a blizzard raging right now and we're a long way from nowhere."

"I guess we should have listened to Moms," Brian said.

"And left Reddy out here to die?" Trixie asked scornfully.

"Of course not," Jim said placatingly, "but we *are* in a bad spot. I don't even know where the main path is now, do you?"

Trixie looked about her and shook her head.

"It's getting darker and darker, too," she said.

"We'll try going in this direction," Jim said and flashed his light. "Put your head down, Trixie, and you won't get the full force of the wind."

"Let's stay close together, all of us," Brian said. "We can't afford to get separated. Coming, Trixie?"

Reddy cried plaintively in Brian's arms.

"I'm coming, and we *will* find a way out!" Trixie answered, her voice vigorous and sure.

"That's the girl!" Jim answered. Then he stumbled and fell in the snow.

Chapter 10
A Caller in the Night

"Jim's hurt!" Trixie cried to Brian. They had been walking along the path single file, with Trixie between the two boys.

"What happened?" Brian asked as he pushed Trixie aside to bend over Jim.

"He stumbled over something and fell," Trixie said. "Watch out!"

She was too late. Brian went down headfirst over Jim's body.

"Brian!" Trixie called frantically. "Jim!"

On the ground they were both making queer choking noises. The swift swirling snow obscured everything around them, even the trees close by.

Terror-stricken, Trixie circled the fallen boys. "Jim!" she called. "Oh, he's been killed!"

"I'm not dead," Jim said, gurgling, "but if you can't get this elephant to roll himself off me, I may be."

"Then why are you making such queer noises, as though you can't get your breath? Brian, too," Trixie added, her voice tense with anxiety.

"Can't you tell laughing when you hear it?" Brian asked, getting up and brushing the snow from himself, only to have it replaced by more. "I like the way you called out to Jim, too, Trixie. Fine sister you are, you weren't concerned when I fell."

"I was, too," Trixie said, exasperated, "but you picked a queer time to be funny and play tricks." She was furious at both of them. "We may not even be alive an hour from now unless we can get under cover someplace. Just think, it's black dark, and Moms must be terribly worried because we aren't home. I can't stand much more of this storm."

"You may be right about it's not being any time to play jokes," Jim said, "but it isn't any time to cry, either. What do you suppose made us both stumble? I can't see an inch ahead of myself." He picked up his flashlight where it had fallen.

Reddy, who had jumped from Brian's arms when he stumbled, rubbed his wet body against Brian's legs, whimpered, and held up his sore paw.

"I know it hurts, fella," Brian said. "I can't do anything about it right now, though. Trixie, we're really up against it. There *must* be a shelter of some kind around here."

"There is!" Jim cried excitedly. His flashlight

hunted around on the ground near him. "It was a log walk that I fell over. Unless I miss my guess it leads to some kind of refuge. That's it, see? Right ahead!" The boys forced the door of a log house that stood on the edge of a small clearing. The fury of the storm drove girl, boys, and dog inside, then slammed the door with mighty force.

"Just in time!" Trixie panted, exhausted.

Jim's flashlight danced around the room. There was no furniture . . . yes . . . along the wall were three old benches piled high with heavy feed sacks.

"Mr. Maypenny must use this for a place to store provisions for the animals and birds," Jim said. "Sure thing, it's an old schoolhouse. Mr. Maypenny used to go to school here himself. Jeepers, it's cold!"

Brian's flashlight had been seeking out corners, too. "There's a stove!" he cried. "Looks like a wood burner!"

"No wood for it, though," Jim said. "None that I can see. Do you see any, Trixie?"

"Not yet," Trixie said, her own flashlight seeking *anything* they could use. "There's a lantern!" She picked it up. "And a folder of matches right by it!" she said, as she snapped the light and lit the lantern. She swung its yellow light around into corners hunting stored wood.

There were only two or three logs near the stove.

"There *must* be a woodpile nearby," Jim said. "I'll go out to see if I can find it."

He opened the door, but the wind roaring through the opening threw him back into the room.

"You can't go out there," Trixie said. "You'd never find your way back. You'd freeze to death!"

"Where do you think you'd rather freeze," Brian asked, "inside or outside? There isn't much difference. I'll go."

"Nobody will go out in this storm," Trixie said determinedly. "We'll burn the benches."

"Just three of them?" Jim asked. "How long would they last? And what would we use to chop them up? No, we'll have to find the woodpile."

Trixie pulled off her mittens, blew on her fingers to warm them, thinking all the while. Suddenly an idea came to her. "I heard old Brom telling Bobby a story the other day about a storm," she said. "Let me think—what did he say they did? Oh, yes, he told about getting wood from outside. Let me see . . . one man would stand just outside the house, and the other man tied the end of a rope around his waist. If the first man got lost before he could find the wood, he would pull on the rope to let the other one know, and *he'd* pull him back to safety."

"We can try it!" Jim exclaimed. "Only where will we find a rope?"

There was no sign of a rope around the old schoolroom. There was nothing but some twine used to tie the feed sacks.

"That idea is out," Jim said. "Think of something else, Trixie. It'll have to be quick, too, because it must be almost zero in this room right now."

Jim blew his breath out. It came back to him in a cloud of steamy vapor.

"The school bell!" Trixie exclaimed. "It must have a rope! Right over there in the corner, Jim, back of you, in that little closet. Open the door!"

Jim opened the narrow door. There hung the frayed rope that was attached to the bell! Inside the small closet there was a narrow ladder. Jim climbed it, unfastened the rope, and dropped it to the floor.

"It's almost worn through in several places," Brian said, running it through his hands. "We'll have to try it, though, Jim. Let's go!"

Each boy wanted to be the one to go out into the storm. They could only decide by drawing lots, so Trixie held two pieces of straw. Jim drew the shorter one.

"I'll fasten this end of the rope around my waist," Brian said, "and stand right there outside the door."

"I'll put the other one around my waist," Jim said.

Outside it were as though an angry giant had wrapped his great arms around the little schoolhouse trying to crush its sides and frosting its panes with his icy breath. Jim, caught up in the rush of wind, waved his arm gallantly and shouted, "Geronimo!" as he dashed into the storm.

While the talk had been going on, Reddy had rushed nervously back and forth across the room in front of the door. When Brian and Jim went out, he tried to dart ahead of them, but Trixie caught and held him. "You stay with me," she commanded. "Down, Reddy!"

Before he left Jim had fastened his wrist watch around Trixie's wrist. Seconds ticked away . . . minutes. . . . From time to time Trixie opened the door a crack to speak to Brian.

He and Jim had arranged a signal. If Jim found the woodpile he would jerk once on the rope. If he wanted to come back, he would jerk twice.

"Did you feel any motion on the rope yet?" Trixie asked Brian.

"Nothing," he answered and huddled against the house. "Of course it slackens and tightens as he goes through the blizzard. It's like the North Pole out here, Trixie. Go back indoors!"

Trixie turned. .

"Wait!" Brian shouted. "There's a jerk! Eureka, he's found the wood! It won't be long now till we have a fire. Go in and twist some of those empty paper bags that held bird seed, Trixie. Make a bed of them in the stove and we can kindle the wood chunks Jim will bring."

Trixie hurried to do his bidding, then waited. Seconds ticked by . . . minutes . . . Jim did not come back.

"Where is he?" Trixie called through the door to Brian.

"I don't know . . . the rope seems slack. . . . I just don't know, Trixie," Brian said and began slowly to pull the rope back. Soon he held up a dangling frayed end.

"It broke!" Brian said, despair choking his voice. "Jim's out there someplace, and he can't find his way back!"

Frantically they both shouted with all their strength, "Jim! Jim! Jim . . . Jim!"

The angry wind, triumphant, threw their voices back to them in a ghoulish echo.

"I'll go after him," Brian said, throwing the rope from him.

"You'll do nothing of the sort!" Trixie said. "You'd just get lost, too. There *must* be some way, Brian . . .

some way! Couldn't we make a loud noise? A horn, maybe . . . that's silly, there isn't any. . . . One of those old pans Mr. Maypenny left here for feeding. . . . I could beat on that. . . . No, I know what I'll do!"

Trixie was across the room in a flash and up the narrow ladder in the closet that led to the bell.

Once at the top, she swung the bell in its cradle. Back and forth, back and forth.

"Clang! Cling-clang! Clang! Clang! Jim! Jim!— Jim!—Jim!—Jim!—JIM!"

"Hallooooo!"

Was it the wail of the wind?

"Halloooo!"

No. It was Jim!

Covered with snow even to his eyelids, Jim stumbled through the door and dropped an armload of wood on the floor.

"It's—not—very—far," he said, panting. "A big— pile of it—but the rope broke. How did you happen to think about ringing the bell?" he asked, a smile breaking over his frosted, reddened face.

"We didn't, at first," Trixie confessed. "I don't know why we didn't. We thought of beating pans and things, then suddenly we remembered the bell."

Jim had recovered his breath. "Start a fire going

with this wood I've brought, Brian," he said. "In a few minutes I'll go out after some more."

"No, you start the fire. I'll go out this time," Brian said.

Jim shook his head. "I know where the woodpile is, Brian. You don't. At least I know the direction to start. It's pretty close to the schoolhouse. If the noise of the storm hadn't been so loud—keep ringing the bell if I don't come back soon."

In spite of Brian's protest Jim tied the rope around his waist and started back. Trixie had doubled the rope so that if one strand broke the other might hold. This time, too, it was she who took up the post outside the door. Brian built the fire.

Back and forth Jim went successfully until a heap of wood stood inside the door. When the small wood stove burned bright and the red isinglass in the window on its door sent a rosy light into the darkened corners, the small schoolhouse seemed cozy and warm.

"Nine o'clock," Trixie said and loosened Jim's wrist watch to give it back to him. "Brian, I *wish* we had some way to let Moms know we are safe. She's alone at the house with Bobby and Mart. I hope Mart doesn't get the idea of starting out to look for us. Moms wouldn't let him, though. I *wish* Daddy were home."

"That's what bothers me most of all," Brian said. "The wind seems to have slackened. Don't you think I'd better make a run for it?"

"No!" Jim's voice was stern, decisive. "No one in this place is going to leave tonight."

"You don't need to be so commanding," Brian said. "You know how Moms will worry."

"Of course I do," Jim said, "and I know that my mother is worrying, too, and Honey, but there isn't a thing they can do or we can do until daylight. My dad's in the city, too. I know this, though, and you should know it, too. Your mother and my mother have confidence in us and will be pretty sure we can take care of ourselves and Trixie."

"She won't *know* it, though," Trixie said, tears coming unbidden to her eyes, "and Moms is *so* good to us. She'll be afraid we don't have anything to eat."

"We don't," Brian said, glad to change the subject before Trixie broke down. "Let's look into the bird seed situation. If it's for the birds, it could be for us, too."

"Sure," Jim said. "I'll go get some snow to melt on top of the stove, and Trixie, you stir up a delicious porridge with some of the latest thing in cereal—bird seed."

"We'll pretend it's one of Moms' casseroles," Trixie said, never sad for long, and entering into the game. "I'm stirring up chicken and noodles," she said, setting a scrubbed pan on the stove, and stirring the bird seed into the water. "Can't you smell the noodles bubbling in the good broth?"

"Help!" Brian cried. "I can *really* smell chicken, but the letdown is going to be too much when I taste it."

"Here's your share, Reddy," Trixie said and fixed a bowl for the big red setter, cooling it for him with fresh snow. "He acts so queer, Brian, don't you think? He keeps running back and forth in front of the door."

"Probably smells a rabbit," Jim said.

"He likes the bird seed anyway," Brian said. "I don't think the storm is quite so severe. I'll take a look."

He opened the door and in a flash Reddy was through it, bounding away through the huge drifts.

No command could bring him back. They called and called, but heard no answering bark.

"It must have been a rabbit, as you said, Jim," Trixie said.

"I was just joking," Jim said. "Even a bird dog couldn't smell a rabbit in this snowstorm. He's gone, though. He'll come barking around the place later, see if he doesn't."

"I wonder," Trixie said. "Do you think he could have gone to get help for us?"

"Gosh, I don't know," Brian said. "He's a pretty smart dog."

"Moms will be even more worried if Reddy shows up without us. Why *couldn't* Mr. Maypenny have a telephone in this place?"

"So he could talk to the animals?" Jim inquired. "Be yourself, Trixie. Let's play Twenty Questions. We're stuck here till morning, and we might as well make the best of it. Think of a subject, Trixie."

Trixie, a little ashamed, brushed her hand over her eyes. "I've something in mind," she said.

"Animal, vegetable, or mineral?" Brian asked.

For a while the game went on. Outside the wind slackened, whined around the schoolhouse, and finally died to a whisper. There was no sound of barking, no sign of Reddy. Trixie, her eyes drooping with the warmth of the fire, blurred the words in trying to play the game.

"I'll pull one of the benches over to the fire," Jim said, aware of Trixie's exhaustion. "It'll be better than sitting on this dirty, hard, cold floor."

He and Brian pushed the heavy feed sacks off a bench, drew it to the fire. "You can rest here till daylight," Jim said.

"I won't even try to rest unless you and Brian do," Trixie said, her eyes nearly closing.

So Jim and Brian unloaded the other two benches and drew them close to the other side of the stove.

The boys stretched their tired lengths, and soon their heavy breathing told Trixie they were sound asleep.

It wasn't so easy for her. Pictures of home, of Bobby, her mother and her worry about their welfare, the concern of the Wheeler family—Honey just adored her new brother Jim—Reddy, and his strange escape into the snow, a lingering horror of Jim's narrow escape when the rope had broken—all these thoughts crowded sleep from Trixie's weary mind and body.

The quiet was so profound that Trixie could hear the ticking of Jim's wrist watch. Gradually she became aware of another sound—outside—muffled—crackling twigs—movement—Reddy?

Reddy, of course.

Trixie slipped from her bench and went to the window. The warmth of the stove had melted the frost enough so she could see through. The clouds had dispersed and a wan moon sent a white path of light through the snow.

Trixie, peering through the window, could see no sign of Reddy. She did see something else. Just leaving the clearing, a dark shape waddled off into the wood. An animal? A man? That was ridiculous. No man would be in the woods on a night like this. What could it be then?

Frightened, Trixie turned back into the room to arouse the boys. They slept so peacefully.

They'd just make fun of me, she thought. *They'd say I was imagining things. Maybe they're right. Mart says my bump of imagination is overdeveloped. Maybe—maybe—he's—right.* Trixie yawned, stretched, and fell exhausted onto the bench, drew the collar of her coat across her eyes, and slept.

A rosy light from the rising sun filled the room and wakened the boys.

"Look at the morning!" Jim cried. "The sun is out. There isn't a cloud in the sky. We can get out of here. I'll stoke the fire to warm us well before we leave."

"Do you want more porridge?" Trixie asked, rubbing her sleepy eyes.

"Not on your life," Brian answered. "Not with Moms' pancakes waiting at home."

"I thought I heard Reddy in the night," Trixie said. "I heard something anyway—then I saw something."

"A raccoon, perhaps," Brian said, "maybe a wolf, or, more likely, a big lump of your vivid imagination."

"It wasn't that," Trixie said, as she wrapped her

wool scarf tight around her head. "Let's hurry and get started for home."

She stepped briskly out into the snow. There in the path, almost close enough to trip over it, lay a bundle wrapped in a tattered quilt.

"What do you suppose it is?" Trixie asked. "And where did it come from?"

Jim poked it gingerly with his toe. "A raccoon couldn't have left it, Brian," he said. "As impossible as it seems, Trixie, you really must have heard someone outside this schoolhouse toward morning." He pulled back the quilt and there, good as new, lay the carved oak lap desk!

Even as they lifted it up to be sure it was real, Reddy, barking furiously, bounded up.

Close behind him came Regan, then Tom, from the Manor House, struggling through the drifts.

"Are you all right?" Regan called. "Is Trixie all right? Jim? Brian? All well?"

"We're fine," Trixie called out happily. "We were just starting for home. How did you find us?"

"I got worried because Jim hadn't come back with Jupiter," Regan said. "I knew he wasn't riding around in the heavy snow. Just about that time your mother called, Trixie, and said that Reddy had come back and was barking and acting strangely."

Trixie put an arm around Reddy's neck and rubbed her face against his warm neck. "Moms must have been frantic," she said.

"She was pretty worried," Regan admitted. "She didn't know which way to turn. She thought we should call the police and organize a searching party, but I persuaded her to let just Tom and me hunt for you. I was sure Reddy was trying to lead us to you."

"How about *my* mother?" Jim asked anxiously.

"I didn't tell her you had Jupiter," Regan said, "until after Mrs. Belden called. Then she wanted to call your father in New York."

"Gee, I hope she didn't do that," Jim said. "There wasn't anything he could do about it."

"I finally convinced her of that, and asked her to let Tom and me have a try first," Regan said. "Tom took Celia down to Crabapple Farm to stay with your mother, Trixie, and we picked up Reddy. We had a hard time keeping Mart from coming, too. I guess we should have let him, but you realize we had to do some wandering around before we found you."

"Poor Moms," Trixie said. "She's had a worse night than we've had, and Mrs. Wheeler and Honey, too. We'd better get started right back so she'll know we're safe."

"Better than that," Regan said. "I arranged a signal

to let them know at Crabapple Farm and at the Manor House just as soon as we found you and knew you were all right. Stand back, everyone!"

They all crowded back against the log school-house and Regan took his shotgun from under his arm, aimed it high in the air, and fired three times. Then he repeated it.

"They'll all be glad to hear that," Regan said. "You kids had better eat something before we start back. Mrs. Belden sent some hot soup in this Thermos and some sandwiches."

"We can't be very far from the valley," Jim said, "if they could hear that gun."

"You're not," Regan said. "You must have wandered around in a circle. We did the same thing hunting for you. You're just at the edge of the pie-shaped clearing Mr. Maypenny owns. Right across there, not more than three hundred yards away, is Maypenny's house, waiting and ready to give you shelter, even if he is away."

Jim pulled off his cap, threw it down in disgust. "A fine woodsman I am," he said, "after all that time I lived in the forest, too, when I ran away from my stepfather. Good Reddy," he said to the red setter who had been running around jumping up on all their knees, and licking their hands. "Good Reddy! We started out to try to find you and you saved us instead."

"Do they give Carnegie medals to dogs?" Brian asked, his voice husky. "Here's one that rates one, if they do."

Chapter 11
The Mask Comes Off

A few days after the storm, Trixie was helping her mother clear away the breakfast dishes. Bobby, in his robe, still sat at the table.

The big kitchen was fragrant with the aroma of coffee, buttered toast, and steaming oatmeal.

The night of the blizzard, faced with but primitive necessities for comfort, Trixie had thought of the cozy Belden kitchen. Then her mind had turned to little children in far-off countries, little children who didn't even have the grain and water she and Jim and Brian had had to eat.

"I hope with all my heart that our UNICEF benefit is a success, Moms," she said. "We'll have to work harder than ever. I wish everyone could have a breakfast like this."

"Don't everybody?" Bobby asked, his mouth full of buttered toast and jam.

"No, lamb," Trixie said.

"Why?"

"It's a little hard for you to understand, Bobby," she

said. "Some day you will. When I think," she said, "about all the people who don't have enough to eat, and how hungry we were in just the short time we were without food . . ."

"I don't even want to think about it," her mother said.

"I do," Bobby said. "I wish I'd been there. I'd have caught that burglar who bringed back the desk. I'll bet it was the same one who stealed it from us, Trixie. I'll bet it was that big boy."

"What big boy?" Trixie asked.

"That big boy who shoveled snow—you know, Trixie, at Mrs. Vanderpoel's house. Brom saw him. He runned away."

"Brom ran away?" Trixie asked, puzzled. "Why did Brom run away?"

"Brom didn't run away, stupid!" Bobby said.

"Bobby!" Mrs. Belden warned.

"It was that big boy who runned away, Trixie," Bobby said. "The one who asked me how much the desk costed."

"What?" Trixie asked. "What did you tell him, Bobby?"

"I told him a hunnerd dollars!"

"That isn't true. It isn't worth that much. That

doesn't matter, though. What did the big boy look like?"

"He looked like a big boy," Bobby said. "An'," he boasted, "I told him Mrs. Vanderpoel had lots and lots of other things she was goin' to give the Bob-Whites, trillions of dollars' worth."

Trixie left the dishes she had started to wash and went over to Bobby's chair.

"What did the big boy say then?" she asked seriously.

"He didn't say anything," her little brother answered. "He just runned away, I told you."

"What do you think of that, Moms?" Trixie asked.

"I don't think a thing about it," her mother answered. "And please don't think about it yourself. I can see that detective gleam in your eye. After all the worry I've had about the blizzard, I'd appreciate a little calm and quiet. It was nothing but idle curiosity on the boy's part. Forget it."

That was an impossible prescription for Trixie. Try as hard as she could, she couldn't even remember seeing a boy shoveling Mrs. Vanderpoel's walks the day the desk was stolen. It was a good thing, she thought, that she had never told Mrs. Vanderpoel what happened to her and Bobby on the way home that day. Now the desk was back as good as ever and what difference did it make where it had been in the meantime? Spider had thought it was a joke. Maybe he thought Tad had taken it. No, Tad didn't know the woods as well as she and Brian and Jim did. He would never have been out in that blizzard. "It's a mystery to me," Trixie said to herself, "a *real* mystery."

Just then the telephone rang. Mrs. Belden answered it.

Now and then she would say, "Goodness, is that so?" or "What did you do then?"

"It was Mrs. Vanderpoel," Mrs. Belden said when she finally dropped the receiver into its cradle.

"Oh, I know," Trixie said, "she told me to come over and look at the George the Third silver she had taken from her grandfather's chest. She said if I wanted to polish it we could show it in our antique show. I guess I'd better go over there now."

"That wasn't what she wanted, Trixie," her mother said seriously. "Last night someone tried to break into Mrs. Vanderpoel's home."

"Oh dear, I hope they didn't scare her too much."

"It didn't frighten her a bit," Mrs. Belden said. "I think it was the other way around. She has real Dutch courage. She said she just took down her father's rifle and stood in the full light of that half-glass door and shouted, 'If you come one step nearer I'll blow the top of your head off!' "

"Oh, Moms, did he scram then?" Bobby asked, all ears and eyes.

"I forgot you were here," his mother answered. "Of course he 'scrammed,' as you say. Wouldn't you?" She ruffled the hair on Bobby's head.

"It's all because of our antique show, I know," Trixie said worriedly. "She's never been bothered before, and she's had all those beautiful things in her house for years. Do you mind if I go over there for a while, Moms?"

"No, I don't think you'd better go just now," her mother said.

"Oh, Moms, we just *have* to have that silver ready for the show. Are you bothered about what happened there last night?"

"Of course I am," her mother answered. "But then, Mrs. Vanderpoel said she had called Spider to tell him about it."

"Then you don't need to worry if Spider's on the job. May I go, Moms?"

"I guess so—yes," her mother said.

"I go, too," Bobby said.

"I think not . . . not till you're entirely well, Bobby.

That's what the doctor said, you know . . . stay inside till you are quite well." Mrs. Belden brought the checkerboard out and put it on the table. "We'll play a game, Bobby," she said.

"I'm well now. I don't want to play checkers. I want to go visiting. I want to go with Trixie. Nobody comes to play with me. I'm tired of staying home," Bobby wailed.

"I don't blame him," Mrs. Belden said to Trixie. "Don't stay too long. Maybe you can do something to amuse him when you come back."

"Where are Brian and Mart?" Trixie asked. "Mart is able to amuse Bobby sometimes when no one else can."

"They went to the clubhouse to work on the furniture Mrs. Vanderpoel gave the B.W.G.'s," Mrs. Belden said.

"That's where I should be," Trixie said, "but I'll be helping the show if I go and look at the silver."

"Why don't you polish it while you're there?" Mrs. Belden asked.

"That's an idea, Moms. I'll call Honey and Diana and ask them to go with me."

The girls were glad to be asked to do something aside from making dolls and aprons. They had a gay assortment of both now, on the shelf at the clubhouse, ready for the show. Most of them were made from remnants donated by the stores in Sleepyside.

It wasn't long after the girls came down the hill that the three of them were walking along Glen Road to the byroad that led to Mrs. Vanderpoel's home.

"It's a mystery about that desk," Diana said. "Who could possibly have left it outside the door at night in the middle of the blizzard?"

"Are you sure it wasn't there when you went into the old schoolhouse?" Honey asked. "It was dark, wasn't it?"

"Yes, but I'm positive it wasn't there," Trixie declared. "As positive as I am that I'm alive. Why, I stumbled over the desk, practically, when I went out the door in the morning. I couldn't have missed it the night before."

"I could believe you missed it easier than I can believe that somebody knew you were in that old school-house and went through the blizzard to return the desk," Honey said. "It just doesn't make sense."

"What happened last night doesn't make sense either," Trixie said and she told them about the attempted robbery at Mrs. Vanderpoel's home.

"That proves one thing," Honey said, "that thieves are on the trail of the antiques we are trying to get together for our show. They're the same ones that were after the desk. But, jeepers, who brought it back?"

"You figure it out," Diana said. "We haven't said a word to anyone about the things in Mrs. Vanderpoel's house. Jim said we shouldn't talk about them, and I know that not one of the B.W.G.'s has said a word. How did the news get out?"

"Bobby had to sound off to a boy who was shoveling snow the day we tried to take the desk home," Trixie said. Then she told them of her conversation with Bobby.

"Gleeps, then that's why you were hijacked," Diana said.

"Exactly," Trixie agreed. "Thank heaven Mrs. Vanderpoel told Spider about last night."

"Yes," Honey said. "It isn't safe for her to be there alone."

"She surely knows how to handle a gun," Trixie said, laughing. "Can't you just see her telling that burglar she'd shoot?"

"I still don't think a woman of her age should be in that house alone," Honey said. "It's all our fault, too, because she wants to help us with our show."

At Mrs. Vanderpoel's house the girls collected the beautiful silver coffee service, the George III tankards,

old flat pieces of silver handmade by eighteenth century silversmiths. The girls spread newspapers on the kitchen table and carried the silver there to be polished.

Mrs. Vanderpoel did not seem greatly disturbed by the happening of the night before. She said that she and her ancestors had lived in that house for more than a hundred years and nothing had ever happened to any of them. "Nothing's going to happen now," she assured them vehemently. "The way that scalawag ran off last night showed he was mighty scared. I'd have shot him and he knew it."

While the girls were busy around the kitchen table, Spider came to the door. Tad was with him. Timidly the boy acknowledged the girls' warm greeting. They had promised Spider that they would be more cordial to Tad and had been trying to keep their word. Tad did not quite know what to make of it.

"I understand you had a visitor last night," Spider said.

"Indeed I did," Mrs. Vanderpoel said with spirit. "He didn't stay long, though. I talked to him down the muzzle of my rifle. He understood what I was saying."

"That's all very well," Spider said, "but some of his gang may try to come back here again. I don't think you should stay out here on this byroad all by yourself."

"How about letting me stay here with you?" Tad asked eagerly.

"There's no need of that, Tad," Mrs. Vanderpoel said. "I'd like right well to have your company, but I can take care of myself no matter who comes, and don't you get it into your head, Spider Webster, that I can't."

Spider chuckled. "Good for you!" he said.

Tad looked longingly around the kitchen, the old wood cook stove, the bright sugar and cooky jars, and sighed. Then he pulled up a chair and helped the girls polish the silver. He carried the finished pieces to the sink, washed them in warm suds, and dried them.

In the meantime Spider scouted around outside the house for footprints, inspected the doorframe, and concluded that Mrs. Vanderpoel had not let the burglar get near enough to leave any evidence. "I'll go along now," he said, "but we'll keep an eye on things. I'd feel a lot better if you'd let Tad stay here."

"I like the boy," Mrs. Vanderpoel said, "and he's welcome any time he comes here, but I'm not going to be mollycoddled by anyone. Come again some other time, Tad, just any time you want, but go along now with Spider."

"I think I'd better go, too," Honey said. "I have a lot

of studying to do, and we're almost through polishing the silver."

"I'll go with you," Diana said. "I promised my mother I'd look after my little sisters."

Trixie stayed to finish the polishing. She was so interested in her work and the stories Mrs. Vanderpoel told her about the different pieces and how they came into her family that she did not notice the growing dusk outside.

"Jeepers," she said when Mrs. Vanderpoel turned on the light, "I'd better go. I told Moms I'd help her with Bobby if Mart couldn't, but here I am now and it's almost dinnertime."

"You'll not go off in this dusk alone," Mrs. Vanderpoel said. "Why don't you stay the night with me? I have so many things I'd like to show you."

"I don't think Moms would want me to stay all night," Trixie said. "She's still sort of nervous about that blizzard and our escape. She's pretty tired, too, from taking care of Bobby. I'll call her and see if Mart and Brian can come for me."

"I'm sorry you stayed so long," Mrs. Belden told Trixie over the telephone. "I've been expecting you any minute. Mart and Brian are at a Y meeting in Sleepyside. They won't be home till late. Your father is at a meeting of the bank board. He'll come home when the boys do. I don't know when that will be."

"Mrs. Vanderpoel said she'd like to have me stay here all night," Trixie said.

"I don't like that idea either," Trixie's mother said. However, when she talked to Mrs. Vanderpoel and discovered that Spider was keeping an eye on the farmhouse, she decided to let Trixie stay for the night.

After a delicious old-fashioned supper of homemade sausage and fried apples, Trixie had a wonderful time curled up in the corner of the living-room couch looking at an album of Vanderpoel ancestors. Mrs. Vanderpoel's long-sleeved challis nightgown and quilted robe made Trixie look exactly like one of the pictures of the Dutch women. Later, after she had climbed up to the high four-poster bed in the guest room and rubbed her sleepy eyes, she imagined she could see an array of white-capped, pink-cheeked Dutch women around her bed.

Visions of them followed Trixie even into her dreams. When suddenly she was awakened by a strange, muffled noise, she was whisked from the seventeenth century into the present.

There the noise was again—something scraping!

Trixie propped her elbow on her pillow and listened.

The noise came from the direction of the lean-to kitchen. Hastily, but quietly, Trixie slipped her feet into her saddle shoes, pulled the big robe around her, and, without turning on the light, slipped through the dining-room into the dark kitchen.

There was that noise again. A window lifted perhaps? Slowly, stealthily, Trixie opened the door to the lean-to kitchen just a crack.

The man inside saw her, ran across the room, knocking pans here and there, making a frightful noise in his eagerness to get back through the window.

"Get your gun!" Trixie called to Mrs. Vanderpoel. "A burglar! He'll get away!"

Mrs. Vanderpoel came running, shouting at the top of her voice, "Hands up! I'll shoot! Stand back, Trixie. Get behind me. Hands up, you thief!"

The man, confused, struck his head on the side of the window trying to get through and, dazed for a second, hesitated, then plunged . . . right into the arms of Tad!

"I've got him!" Tad called. "Get a rope, Trixie! Help me tie him up!"

Little Mrs. Vanderpoel hurried with a clothesline, and Trixie ran out the door with it to where the man, held fast in Tad's arms, struggled to get away. She

looped the rope around his arms while Tad held them pressed against the man's back. Then they bound the burglar's legs fast.

"*There* you are!" Tad said. "Now we'll see *who* you are!" He pulled the mask from the man's face.

It wasn't a man at all, but a boy not much older than Tad.

"It's the lad who shoveled my walks!" Mrs. Vanderpoel said. "Maybe he just came to collect for his work."

"At this time of night?" Tad asked. "And masked? No ma'am. I know him. It's Bull Thompson."

The boy growled at Tad, "I'll get you for this!"

"That voice," Trixie said. "Why, he's one of the gang who stole the desk. I'm sure I remember his voice. Where did you know him, Tad?"

"He was a member of the Hawks," Tad said, "but not for long. He sure didn't fit into our club. He only joined it to get hold of our funds. He ran off with eleven dollars, too. I haven't seen him for months. I thought he'd moved out of Sleepyside. His uncle, Snipe Thompson, disappeared and I thought Bull went with him. Snipe had a bookie joint over on Hawthorne Street . . . did time for it. Say, Trixie, call the sergeant at the police station. Tell him to find Spider and send him out here in the patrol car. It'll be reform school for you this time, Bull, or I'll miss my guess."

Bull only snarled his answer.

Spider came with Sergeant Molinson, the man who had helped to rescue Trixie and Mart from the trailer when they had been kidnaped. "It's you, again, poison!" the sergeant said to Trixie. "Every time I see you it means trouble."

"Don't you say one word against that girl," Mrs. Vanderpoel warned him, "or Tad, either. I suppose Spider told you to keep a watch, whether I wanted you to or not," she said to Tad. "And you, Sergeant, those kids did a better job on that crook than you policemen could have done."

"Yeah," Sergeant Molinson agreed, "maybe we ought to put 'em on the squad. Come on now, Bull. Into the patrol car with you. We'll have some questions to ask you—been rough-housing the school and stealing from desks and lockers, haven't you?"

"Prove it!" Bull sneered.

"We will, don't worry," Spider said. "We'll get the rest of your gang, too. Do you want to tell us who they are? Is your Uncle Snipe in on it? Spill it, Bull."

"Naw," Bull said, "no smart aleck cop is ever goin' to get that out of me. I don't snitch on pals."

Chapter 12
"This Can't Be I!"

"I can surely breathe easier," Mrs. Belden told Trixie, "when I know that Mrs. Vanderpoel's burglar has been caught. Do you see these gray hairs on my temples?" Mrs. Belden pushed back her hair. "You put them there, Trixie. I've worried more about you than all three of the boys, though I've had plenty of occasions to be concerned about them, too, with all the situations they get involved in with you."

"It isn't my fault if mysterious things happen when I'm around," Trixie said. "How could I help it if that burglar came back to Mrs. Vanderpoel's house when I was there?"

"It would have been just as easy for you to step out in the hall and call the police as it was to go out in that lean-to kitchen all by yourself. Is it any wonder my hair is turning gray when I think of what might happen to you?"

"I never even thought of calling the police," Trixie said. "Anyway, how did I know it wasn't a cat prowling around? You know I had to tell Mrs. Vanderpoel that the desk had been stolen. Do you know what she said?"

"I can't imagine . . . and I never could see why you didn't tell her before."

"I didn't want her to think I was so helpless as to let someone steal it right under my nose. Well, when I told her she said, 'Land sakes, child, I've known about it for a long time. I still know more about it than you do.' What do you suppose she meant by that?"

"Why didn't you ask her?" Mrs. Belden wanted to know.

"I didn't have a chance. Say, Moms, they sent Bull Thompson to reform school. You don't have to worry about him any more."

"They haven't sent the rest of his gang anywhere. Until they do, I'll not have an easy moment. Thank goodness it's only a little over two weeks till your antique show. Then I'll have a rest from worry until you get into some other project," Trixie's mother said.

"Don't be so cross with me, Moms," Trixie said.

"I don't mean to be, but goodness, Trixie, you'll be fourteen years old the first of May, and you've never been content to be a girl instead of a tomboy. You've never even dressed like the pretty girl you are since that cousin of Honey's was here. Maybe after the antique show is over you can plan some real boy and girl parties, and no more detective work."

"That's just what I'm trying to tell you, Moms," Trixie said. "You'll be glad to know that Diana is having a dress-up party at her house Friday evening. It's sort of a pre-Valentine party. Her mother and father are having people in for dinner February fourteenth so Diana is going to have her party early."

"That will mean a new dress for you, Trixie," her mother said, delighted.

"Not a long one, Moms, please. Diana said her party this time isn't going to be the way it was Halloween, when her imitation uncle ruined the whole thing with all that crazy food and hired orchestras."

"I hope it's simpler," her mother said, "because it didn't sound to me like a young people's party at all. Trixie, I'll meet you this afternoon and we'll find a dress for you—shoes, too."

"Heels?" Trixie asked.

"Of course," her mother said, obviously pleased, "as high as you want them."

"I'll have to get shoes, of course," Trixie agreed, "but just forget about the dress. I can wear one of Honey's or maybe one of Diana's. They have closets full of them. Then you can give me the money the dress would cost and I'll add it to the UNICEF fund."

"There are several things wrong with that reasoning," her mother told her. "In the first place I want you to have a pretty dress or two of your own. You hardly own a thing but sweaters and skirts. You're forever wearing Honey's clothes."

"She doesn't care," Trixie insisted.

"This time *I* care," Mrs. Belden said.

"All right, Moms, if you feel that way about it," Trixie said. "Can you pick me up about two thirty? I'll be out of English class then. Maybe Honey and Diana will go with me to get a dress."

"This is to be *our* expedition," Mrs. Belden said. "I want you to have the prettiest dress we can find. Sometimes I think you pay too much attention to what the girls say and haven't an idea of your own about clothes."

"Honey and Diana can put on anything and look beautiful," Trixie said, not at all enviously. "Honey is just gorgeous and you know it. If anything, Diana is prettier. Everyone at Sleepyside High thinks Diana is the prettiest girl in the class."

"I think Trixie Belden is going to give her some competition," Mrs. Belden said.

"You wouldn't be prejudiced would you, Moms?"

Trixie teased. "Have you taken a good look at my freckles lately? And my waist? It's miles around."

"It's nothing of the sort," her mother said, provoked. "That's another thing we'll shop for—a girdle."

"Gleeps, Moms, I'd never wear it, not in a thousand years."

"Just wait and see. We'll get it before you try on dresses. I wish you would take more pride in your appearance."

"Wait just a minute, Moms. You've always told me not to grow up too soon," Trixie said.

"That was two years ago at least," her mother said, exasperated. "I *don't* want you to grow up, but I'd like to be able to tell the difference between you and your brothers without straining my sight."

That afternoon in Sleepyside Mrs. Belden made a few purchases before she picked up Trixie. A girdle was one of them. Before Mrs. Belden and Trixie went into the Teen Town dress department, she first went to the restroom and succeeded, with many a protest from Trixie, in getting her into the girdle. It slimmed her waist amazingly.

"Now we'll look for the dress," Mrs. Belden said.

"Don't even pause at the rack that has pink dresses," Trixie said.

"Why not?" her mother asked. "I've always liked pink. Pink is pretty on blondes."

"Not on this strawberry blonde," Trixie said.

The saleswoman slipped a pink dress over Trixie's head, fastened it, and Trixie turned to her mother. "See what I mean?" she asked.

"Don't slump so. Stand up straight," her mother answered. "You're just trying to make it look as bad as you can. It's a pretty dress."

"The dress is all right," Trixie said. "But look at it with *my* hair, and *my* freckles."

"Pink *isn't* exactly right," her mother agreed reluctantly. "We'll try the blue one, please," she said to the saleswoman.

There was something the matter with the blue one. There was something the matter with the yellow one, with the striped one, with the green one.

"You can't make a swan out of me," Trixie said, laughing. "You should have Honey for a daughter. Sit down here, Moms. I'll look around by myself. You're tired. If I *have* to get a dress I *have* to get one, I guess."

Trixie looked around at all the racks in Teen Town, then she wandered over to the Young Flair shop. *These aren't quite so full-skirted,* she thought. *Maybe I'd look all right in something just a little more streamlined.*

177

She found a dress of white chiffon. It was made very simply, with a Peter Pan collar and short sleeves. The skirt was short, and it *was* very full, but it was stitched in pleats around the hips to hold the fullness in place.

When Trixie slipped it over her head and looked in the mirror she couldn't believe her eyes. "I feel like the old woman in the Mother Goose rhyme," she said to herself. " 'Laws a mercy this can't be I.' I'll show it to Moms."

Her mother's exclamation when she appeared was sufficient approval. "It's the perfect dress," she said. "It's time I turned you loose to select your own clothes. Shall we go and find some white slippers for it?"

"Heavens no, Moms," Trixie said. "I'll get some bright green ones. Then I can wear them this summer with cotton dresses."

Mrs. Belden held her palms up and shrugged. "Green shoes, of course," she said.

When they had finished their shopping, they went into the tearoom for a soda before starting back home.

There they found Diana and her mother at a table and joined them. "We've been shopping for some things for Diana's party," Mrs. Lynch explained, "favors, paper plates, paper cloth, and cups—all Valentine things."

"We've been shopping, too, for the party," Trixie said. "A new dress!" she said excitedly. "I never knew it could be so much fun to buy clothes. I won't even tell you what it's like, Diana. You'll see at the party." Trixie's blue eyes twinkled. "Moms may make a swan out of me yet. That would be a laugh, wouldn't it?"

"I don't know who would laugh," Diana said. "Honey and I keep telling you that you're getting prettier every day."

Trixie reddened and changed the subject. "I'd give anything to know who those other people were who were with Bull Thompson when they stole the desk. Moms is relieved because Bull Thompson is at the reform school, but she's still terribly worried about the others."

"Maybe there aren't any others now, Trixie," Diana said. "Bull Thompson was all alone when he tried to break into Mrs. Vanderpoel's house."

"We *think* he was," Trixie said. "I don't know. Tad said that Bull's Uncle Snipe Thompson is an ex-convict and that Bull had been living with him."

"I might as well give up," Mrs. Belden said. "I thought your mind was miles away from all that burglary business."

"Why, Moms, you know that Honey and I are going

to be detectives some day, and you know very well there are other thieves loose who know all about the antiques we'll have at the show. They read about the jewel box in *The Sleepyside Sun,* and the news story had to go on and tell about a lot of other things we'd have such as—well, the samurai swords, for instance."

"Do you see what I have to put up with?" Mrs. Belden appealed to Mrs. Lynch.

"It makes me nervous, too," Mrs. Lynch said. "I'll be glad when the UNICEF show is over and all the antiques are safely back with the people who own them. Do you honestly want to be a detective some day?" she asked Trixie.

"Indeed I do, more than ever," Trixie said. "If Spider would only help a little more, I think we could find out who those other crooks are, and—"

"Maybe I should be glad that Diana just wants to be a flight stewardess," Mrs. Lynch said, "though it will be a long time yet before the girls really have to decide. I used to shiver when I'd think of the possibility that Diana would be up in the air so much of the time. Maybe the girls will change their minds by the time they finish college."

"Not me," said Trixie, the box with the white chiffon dress forgotten, and the green slippers farthest from her mind. Her thoughts centered about the Bob-White clubhouse in the woods, the antiques they had repaired, and the need for protecting them from the thieves who were still at large.

Chapter 13
Moll Dick Goes Partying

The day of Diana's party a cellophane-topped box was delivered to Miss Trixie Belden. Bobby answered the door and took the box to his mother where she was working in the kitchen.

"It's a corsage," she said. "Trixie will love it. Put it in the refrigerator, Bobby."

"Can't I open the box?" Bobby asked, his eyes popping.

"Of course not. It's Trixie's," his mother said.

"I'll bet Daddy sent it, 'cause he sent a box like this to you on your birthday," Bobby said.

"I doubt if Daddy sent this one," his mother answered.

"Guess what's in the refrigerator!" Bobby called out to Trixie as she got off the school bus.

"I don't know, Bobby," Trixie said. "A lemon meringue pie?"

"No, sir," Bobby answered, giggling. "It's not to eat. It's to smell."

"A bunch of green onions," Trixie guessed.

"No, sir!" Bobby said again.

"I'll just see for myself," Trixie said and open refrigerator door.

"It's an orchid!" she exclaimed. "A white one—see, Moms—on a red satin heart—who could have sent me an orchid?" Excitedly she took the little card out of the envelope and read:

Dear Moll Dick: Is this your first orchid? I hope so. See you tonight.

> Jim.

Trixie blushed to the roots of her sandy hair. "Did you ever have an orchid in your life?" she asked her mother. "A beautiful white orchid from—of course you've had them from Daddy—but from a boy?"

"It was gardenias when I was your age," her mother said. "It will look pretty with your new white dress."

"Beautiful!" Trixie said, dancing around the room. "Oh, Moms, take it please and put it back in the refrigerator. Just look at my hair! I brushed it for an hour this morning, and it still looks like a Fiji Islander's hair. And my freckles! May I possibly use just a teeny little bit of your powder base tonight?"

"You may use anything I have," her mother said, "even my lipstick."

"You know you're safe, Moms. I have my own. How can I possibly ever dance in high heels?"

"You'll be dancing on air," her mother said. "You won't notice the heels."

The record player was playing softly when Trixie, with Brian on one side and Mart on the other, walked into the Lynches' beautiful big living-room.

The ceiling and wall lights in the long room were covered with gay Japanese lanterns. In the dining-room bright red cellophane hearts dangled from the chandelier. The table, covered with a Valentine paper cloth, held trays of Cokes, potato chips, popcorn, pickles, olives, and Valentine candies. On a cart a portable oven held hamburgers fresh from the kitchen—plenty of them that were replaced just as fast as the hungry guests could eat them.

Diana's father and mother were busy putting last touches to the room. Through the railing at the head of the stairs as they came in, Trixie saw the four faces of Diana's little twin brothers and twin sisters peeping at the scene below.

"Hi, Cinderella!" Jim said when he caught sight of Trixie. "Some dress! You smell wonderful, too."

"It's Moms' perfume," Trixie said, grinning. "The orchid is super, Jim. Thanks!"

"Trade it for a dance," Jim said and Trixie floated off on tiptoe, heels not even touching the floor, dancing on cloud nine.

Diana had asked Tad to her party. After the burglary at Mrs. Vanderpoel's house, Spider and Tad had gone often, at the little Dutch woman's invitation, to visit her, most of the time to stay for dinner.

After Mrs. Vanderpoel had heard about Spider's attempt to make a home for Tad, trying to cook, manage the house, direct Tad's activities all by himself, she told Trixie, "I need a boy around this house. I love to have someone to cook for. I'm going to ask them if they'd like to come and live with me."

So it had been arranged. For a nominal rental, for Spider would have it no other way, they moved to Mrs. Vanderpoel's house.

Tad now went back and forth on the bus with the other country boys and girls. They were all good friends.

At the Valentine party after Tad danced with Trixie he said, "I guess you know that Bull Thompson was sent to the reform school."

"Yes," Trixie said, "and it wasn't half what he

deserved. Did Sergeant Molinson or your brother find out anything more about the rest of his gang? Was Bull's Uncle Snipe mixed up in it?"

"I don't know," Tad said soberly. "No matter how they questioned Bull they couldn't get a thing out of him. He said the others had skipped to another part of the country. No one can take Bull Thompson's word for anything, though."

"Thank goodness nothing happened to Mrs. Vanderpoel," Trixie said fervently. "I'm glad you and Spider live with her now."

"That goes more ways than one," Tad said. "She's tops."

Jim came up then with Cokes and hamburgers for Trixie and himself. "I should have brought one for you," he said to Tad. "Here, take this and I'll get another."

"No, thanks," Tad said and he jumped up from the chair where he had been talking to Trixie. "I'll get it myself."

"Why didn't you tell me you could dance like a feather?" Jim asked Trixie.

"Mart didn't think so when I was dancing with him," Trixie said, smiling. "He said I punctured his toes with my high heels."

"I feel so sorry for him," Jim said. "I'll tell you this,

I'd lots rather dance with you than I would with Mart. Say, Trixie, why don't we take our food over on that divan that faces the window?"

Trixie followed Jim to the seat in front of the window. In front of them, through the window, the light from the full moon etched shadows of the bare trees on the glistening snow. There were millions of stars in the sky. They could see down the hill toward the Manor House. Back of them in the big living-room the record player played soft music.

Trixie finished her hamburger, then put her head back against the couch and dreamed. Outside the moon seemed to come closer and closer. Watching it, Trixie suddenly jerked her head to awareness.

"That light," she whispered to Jim. "It's Regan with a lantern. He's running toward the clubhouse."

"Shhhh!" Jim warned. "Get your coat. Quiet! I'll meet you at the front door, right outside."

Outside Jim held tight to Trixie's hand to keep her from stumbling in her high heels. Faster and faster they went, trying to catch up with Regan and his bobbing lantern.

"Everybody keeps saying," Trixie gasped, as she ran, "not to worry any more with Bull Thompson in reform school. Regan, did the alarm sound?"

"It sure did," Regan said. "I was down in the stable yard and didn't hear it at first," he panted. "Blast it! There they go down Glen Road!" Red-haired Regan swung the lantern angrily in disgust. "Oh, for a good rifle! I left the apartment for about half an hour and this had to happen!"

"Forget it, Regan," Jim said. "Come on, Trixie, let's see what happened in the clubhouse."

"Just look at this!" Trixie moaned as they went inside, and turned on the light. The beautiful curtains Honey had made had been jerked from the rods, to be used for bags to carry the small articles now piled on them. Everything had been dragged from the shelves, some of it thrown carelessly around the room.

"Go up to your house, Jim," Regan said. "Tell your dad to call Sergeant Molinson and Spider, too, if he can reach him. Ask him to tell them to get out here as quick as they can."

"I smelled gasoline when I came in," Trixie told Regan as Jim left to call his father.

"I'll look around," Regan said, disgusted. "Just look at this, Trixie, gasoline-soaked rags!"

"Oh, heavens," Trixie cried, "do you know what they were going to do, Regan? Set our beautiful clubhouse on fire after they robbed it! Thank goodness for that alarm. It scared them away before they could steal anything."

"You can't be sure of that, Trixie, till you take an inventory," Regan said. "Here comes the whole gang from the Valentine party now."

Tad, eager to help, seemed to be everywhere. He helped Mart gather up the gas-soaked rags into a pile on a cleared place away from the clubhouse. Regan set a match to them.

As they blazed against the sky the crowd stood out as vividly as a painting, the girls in their bright dresses, coats hastily gathered around their shoulders, the boys milling around, thrilled at their first taste of off-TV drama, while far away on Glen Road the police siren screamed.

In the light of the fire Trixie spied something small shining against the snow. She picked it up, turned it over in her hands. "I guess it's Patch's dog tag," she said to herself and put it in her pocket. "I'll ask Jim when I have a chance."

Chapter 14
At the Police Station

During the next few days the Bob-Whites of the Glen worked as they had never worked before, setting the clubhouse to rights. The girls pressed the draperies and put them back on the windows. They rearranged the things they had made on the shelves—dolls and aprons, repainted toys, small framed pictures.

Mart, furious at the scratches on the cherry gate-leg tables, worked and rubbed till the marks disappeared. Finally the clubhouse was in order again.

Only the samurai swords seemed to be missing. Not a trace of them could be found. The burglars must have made off with them.

"It's a shame we didn't sell them to the Hakaito brothers when they wanted to buy them," Brian said. "Now we'll probably never see them again, and they won't do anyone any good."

Trixie didn't think the police were trying very hard to investigate the robbery at the clubhouse. "Why do they have to take forever to find anything out?" she asked the others. "I'd like to do a little investigating myself."

"Lay off it," Mart warned. "You know what Moms and Dad said . . . no more sleuthing."

"I don't have time now before the show," Trixie said, "but if I did, I'd—"

"You'd what?" Mart asked. "Bull Thompson's in the reform school, and he didn't give anyone a single lead on his partners."

"Well, there must be *some* way of finding who they are," Trixie insisted. "I'd feel a lot safer about our show on Saturday if they all were in jail."

She meant it, too, because one or two of the people who had promised Trixie some of their rare antiques had withdrawn their offers in the face of the publicity about the clubhouse.

"Another thing," she said, "no one has ever found out who returned the oak desk the night of the blizzard. I know Bull Thompson didn't have a change of heart. It's a real mystery."

"Maybe one of the other crooks in Bull's gang is a softie and returned it," Mart said.

"That isn't even probable," Trixie said. "Anyone who would put gasoline rags around our clubhouse hasn't any heart at all."

That night after Trixie went to bed she couldn't sleep. Her mind went back to the Valentine party . . . the

192

music, dancing. *It was wonderful,* she thought. *Then that awful time at the clubhouse . . . those gasoline rags . . . that fire might have been our club burning. I wish the police could trace those crooks.*

All at once a thought struck her. "Jeepers," she said to herself, "I forgot all about that dog tag I found. It isn't Reddy's. Maybe it's not even Patch's tag. If it isn't, it *might* be a clue! I'll ask Jim about it tomorrow."

On the bus the next morning Trixie asked Jim to meet her in the library at study period. When he did, she took the metal disk from her pocket, turned it numbered side up, and asked, "What is this, Jim, a dog tag? Did it come off of Patch's collar? It doesn't belong to Reddy."

"One thing at a time, Trixie," Jim said. "It isn't Patch's tag. It isn't a dog tag at all. It's the number of an automobile."

"An automobile?" Trixie asked excitedly. "Then it *is* a clue. It belongs to one of the crooks who stole the swords!"

"What *are* you talking about?" Jim asked.

"The night of the robbery at the clubhouse," Trixie said, as she rubbed the disk to show the number better, "I found this on the ground outside."

"Why didn't you show it to someone before?" Jim asked, exasperated. "I wish you wouldn't try to do so many things on your own. If the police had had it, they might have been able to trace the car long before this."

"Don't be mad at me, Jim. I didn't know it had anything to do with the car the thieves used."

"You could have tried to find out what it was before this. Come on, let's go and use the public telephone."

"You aren't going to call the police and give them my clue, are you, Jim?" Trixie asked.

"It isn't *your* clue, Trixie, and the police are sure enough going to have to know about this key ring tag. I'm going to call the Motor Registration Bureau over at the county seat, and see if they can tell me who owns the car with this number."

Meekly Trixie followed Jim out into the hall and listened while he called.

She heard him ask for information, listen for an answer. "I have a good legitimate reason for wanting to know it," she heard Jim say.

When he turned away from the telephone, however, she could tell from the look on his face that he hadn't been given the information.

"They say they never give it over the telephone," Jim said, "only to insurance companies and the police."

"Then we'll just have to go and see Sergeant Molinson after school," Trixie said.

"*You* don't have to go," Jim said. "*I* can go."

"Like fun you will," Trixie said. "It's *my* clue, and if you think for one minute, Jim Frayne, that you're going there without me—"

"Calm down, calm down, smooth your hair back, Trixie," Jim said. "I just thought you'd have to help your mother, or do some work at the club."

"There isn't anything I have to do to help Moms, and most of the work is done at the club," Trixie said.

"Come along, then," Jim said.

But it wasn't that easy. When Jim and Trixie told the rest of the B.W.G.'s they were going to do an errand in town after school, Mart was suspicious.

"It's another one of Trixie's 'cases,' as she calls them," Mart said. "*I* have another name for them."

"It'll be a big word no one can understand," Trixie said.

"Just try to remember, Trixie Belden," Honey said, "that we are *all* members of the Bob-Whites of the Glen. If you know something about that robbery that the rest of us don't know, you'd better tell us."

"Yes," Diana said, "it seems to me you're getting so you think you know everything, and want to do everything yourself. You're not even any fun any more."

"I don't know what you're talking about," Trixie said, perplexed.

"We're talking about just what it is you have to do after school tonight that you can't tell the rest of us," Mart said. "Spill it, Trixie."

"If you are all going to be mad at me I might just as well tell you," Trixie said. "It's just that I found this tag the night of the fire. I thought it was a dog tag and that maybe it belonged to Patch. Jim says it's a key ring tag and probably this number on it will tell us who owned the car the thieves made off in. We were going down to the police station to have them call the Motor Registration Bureau for information."

"Then we'll just go right along with you," Mart said. "We wouldn't want to deprive you of our company, would we?" he asked the other B.W.G.'s.

"We wouldn't think of it," they chorused.

"We won't be taking the bus," Diana said over her shoulder to the bus driver who held the door open.

"You call Moms," Trixie said to Brian, "please. She'll think everything is all right if *you* call her and tell her we'll be a little late."

"Don't bother to call," Honey said. "Tom is going to bring Mother in to the station to take the train to meet Daddy in New York. I'll tell him to pick us up at the schoolhouse. We'll get home about the same time we would if we took the bus."

So it was arranged.

On the way to the police station the Bob-Whites passed the small retail store where the Hakaito brothers sold the produce they raised in their outlying farms and greenhouses.

Kasyo was in the window arranging a display. When he saw the Bob-Whites pass, he waved to them frantically, and called back to his brother Oto. Together they threw open the door, grinning and bowing.

Inside, Oto pulled out a bench and some chairs.

"Please to sit down," he invited.

"We're sorry, Oto," Jim said, "but we have to hurry over to the police station."

"Won't take long," Oto said. "Maybe have something more to tell police. You miss something from clubhouse the night of Valentine party?" he asked.

Trixie's face fell. "The swords," she said. "Now you'll never be able to buy them for your father and the museum in Tokyo. They were stolen."

"Hakaito brothers *have* swords," Oto replied. "We find them in pawnshop in White Plains. Thief pawn them there."

"He did?" Trixie exclaimed. "Did you ask the

pawnbroker for a description of him?"

"Yes," Oto said sadly. "He said he didn't remember who pawned swords. I do not think he tell the truth."

"Of course he didn't," Mart said. "Those people are always afraid they'll get in bad with the law."

"Maybe the police can help jog his memory," Trixie said. "We're going there now, you know," she said to the Hakaito brothers. "Did you say *you* have the swords now?"

"Yes, Miss Trixie," Oto said. "Hakaito brothers buy samurai swords. We were going to take them to clubhouse tonight, give them back to Bob-Whites of the Glen. Here are your swords!"

Kasyo unrolled the paper from a package he pulled from under the counter and displayed the Satsuma samurai swords, polished and beautiful.

While Mart and Brian and Honey and Diana exclaimed over the return of the swords and chatted with the Japanese brothers, Jim and Trixie, huddled in the background, whispered busily.

"We can't possibly accept the swords, can we?" Jim asked the others, interrupting their conversation.

The Hakaito brothers' faces fell.

"You not accept present?" Oto asked.

"No," Trixie said. "You want those swords to send

to your father. They are yours. They belong in Tokyo. You paid money for them at the pawnshop, money you worked hard to earn."

"Makes no difference," Oto and Kasyo said, then Oto continued, "Money is for little UNICEF children. We give swords. Maybe be lucky enough to buy them back at antique show." They both grinned happily.

"Why not just consider lending them to us for the exhibit?" Jim inquired. "We'd never feel right if you weren't able to send them to your father."

The Hakaito brothers held a conference in quick, sibilant whispers.

"How much you think swords sell for at show?" Oto asked.

"Maybe a hundred dollars for the pair," Trixie said. "I think that is what we planned to ask for them. Why?"

"We pay only fifty dollars," Oto said happily, "at pawnshop! We pay you fifty dollars more, then we own swords, and you exhibit them at show. That right?"

"It's wonderful!" Trixie said. "I'm *so* glad we will have them to display at the antique show."

"You like maybe to show other swords?" Oto asked hesitantly.

"We sure would!" Mart exclaimed. "Do you have others?"

"Yes," Kasyo said, "six other swords. After antique show we send all to Tokyo to our father. We have Japanese prints and carved ivory, too. You like to show them?"

Trixie clapped her hands, delighted. "We'd love it," she said. "Shall the boys pick them up tomorrow?"

"If you like *we* fix exhibit at showroom," Oto said. Kasyo nodded vigorously. "We fix Japanese style," he said.

"That will be swell!" Jim said.

"Keen!" Mart added.

"Thanks a million," Trixie said. "We have to go now. We'll see you at the showroom tomorrow. Good-by!"

"Good-by! Good-by!" the Hakaito brothers said, smiling happily.

At the station Sergeant Molinson groaned when he saw Trixie and her group. "Oh, no," he said, "not again! What is it this time?"

Trixie told him about the Hakaito brothers and the swords; how they had bought them at the pawnshop, and how the man who sold them said he could not remember who brought them in.

"We'll send a man over to inquire," the sergeant

said. "I doubt if it leads to anything. It's hard to get information out of those guys. They seldom ask questions when anything is pawned. We'll look into it right away," he added quickly when he saw Trixie's disappointed face. "Is that all?"

Trixie produced the tag and told of their attempt to get information about it from the Bureau.

"They have to obey the rules," the sergeant said. "We'll see now just what they have over at the Bureau on this license number."

He dialed, waited for the sound of ringing, then repeated the number on the key tag and held the receiver, waiting.

"Yes?" he said. "That's right. No, that's the number on the tag. What did you say? Stolen? When? Yes, that's the night all right. Was it recovered? I see. Thanks."

"That clue led up a blind alley," he told the anxious waiting B.W.G.'s. "The car *was* stolen the night your clubhouse was entered. The White Plains police found it two days later. No harm done. Just out of gas."

"Were there any clues to who stole it?" Jim asked hopefully.

"None at all," Sergeant Molinson said. "It probably *was* the crooks who were trying to break into your clubhouse. The stolen escape car won't help us a bit. I'll hold on to this tag, Trixie. Might as well forget about the car, kids."

"Did he tell you what the car looked like—the man at the Bureau?" Trixie asked.

"Yeah, Trixie, he did," the sergeant said. "It was a blue and white sedan. If you can make anything out of that let us know, will you? There are probably a thousand blue and white sedans that pass here every day. Maybe we should have taken Mrs. Vanderpoel's suggestion after all and added you to our squad."

"Maybe you *do* need help," Trixie said. "Our antique show is the day after tomorrow, you know."

"Don't I know it!" the sergeant exclaimed.

"We will have lots of valuable things in the showroom by tomorrow night," Trixie added.

"Shall I detail the whole squad to watch them?" the sergeant asked sarcastically. "The showroom is on Main Street in plain sight. Your father's bank, Trixie, is right across the street. Is he going to call off the bank guard to watch your showroom? You kids are beginning to get on my nerves. We'll watch the place for you. Scram!"

The sergeant turned on his swivel chair to dismiss them.

Chapter 15
The Most Fun Ever

Tom had the two little Lynch boys, Larry and Terry, in the car with him when he picked up the Bob-Whites.

"This is a surprise," Diana said and hugged her little brothers. "Where did you find them?" she asked Tom.

"Your mother went to New York, too, with Mrs. Wheeler, Diana," Tom explained. "Miss Trask has the little girls with her, and the boys are going to stay at your house for dinner and the evening, Trixie."

"Oh, goody," Trixie said, "Bobby will be happy. He's been so lonesome for someone to play with. Can't you and Honey stay, too," she asked Diana, "and Jim?"

"Your mother is away ahead of you," Tom said. "She told me to dump the whole carload at Crabapple Farm. She'll really have her hands full."

"Not with us to help her," Trixie said. "You don't know my mother. This will be fun. Isn't it wonderful that we have a holiday tomorrow because of Washington's birthday? We can have all day tomorrow to get ready for our antique show and we don't have to think about it tonight. There's Reddy to welcome us. And your dog, too, Jim!"

Reddy and Patch ran out wagging their tails. The two dogs were good friends.

"Down, Patch!" Jim commanded. "Heel!" Patch obeyed immediately.

"It won't do to tell Reddy to get down, or to heel," Mart laughed. "We've never trained him. We just play with him. He minds Bobby now and then when he feels like it."

"Reddy doesn't have to mind anyone all the rest of his life," Trixie said, "not after the way he came home for help for us when we were lost in the blizzard. There's Bobby waving from the window," she said to Terry and Larry. "Run on in, while we collect our books. Won't you come in for a cup of coffee?" she asked Tom.

"Celia would crown me if I did," Tom answered. "We have a chance to have dinner all by ourselves in the trailer tonight, with all the families gone. I'll be back about nine o'clock to pick everyone up."

"That early?" Trixie asked.

"That's an hour past the time Larry and Terry are supposed to go to bed," Diana reminded her. "It'll take almost another hour to get them to bed."

"What difference does it make?" Mart wanted to

know. "Tomorrow's a school holiday for us. Let the kids live it up. How about nine thirty, Diana?"

"All right," Diana said, "nine thirty. Will it be all right for Tom to come then, Honey?"

"If Tom says so," Honey answered.

The whole crowd followed the little boys into the house. Mr. and Mrs. Belden, in the kitchen, greeted them warmly. "Put your wraps in the study," Mr. Belden said. "Your mother has dinner almost ready," he added to Trixie.

Honey and Diana followed Trixie into the kitchen, tied aprons over their sweaters and skirts, and asked to be given something to do.

"You can finish making the Waldorf salad," Mrs. Belden said. "Take this big bowl. The apples are already washed and so is the celery. Chop them, quarter the marshmallows, add them to it, and mix the whole thing together with mayonnaise. Make plenty of it."

"What shall I do, Moms?" Trixie asked. "I know, I'll fix the hamburgers and pat them into cakes."

"Nobody *ever* made better hamburgers than you, Mrs. Belden," Honey said. "How do you do it? They don't taste nearly so good, even at Wimpy's."

"I add a slice of bread, crumbled and soaked in milk, to each pound of meat," Mrs. Belden said. "Then I

season the mixture with salt and pepper and just a little curry powder."

"Bread and milk?" Diana asked, amazed.

"Yes. It keeps the juice in the hamburger patties," Mrs. Belden explained.

"It does something delicious to it," Honey said, dicing the apples and putting them into the bowl. "I love to cook."

"You don't have much chance to practice it, do you, with such a good cook as you have? There are times when *I'd* like to have a cook," Mrs. Belden said.

"This isn't one of them, is it, Moms?" Trixie asked.

"No indeed, not with such good helpers as I have. When you finish that, Trixie, you may spread the cream on the pumpkin pies. It's whipped and in the refrigerator. Make plenty of hamburgers, though!"

"You'll never ask Larry and Terry again when you see the way they consume hamburgers," Diana said. "Listen to that yelling! I hope they don't break anything."

"Our living-room is child-proof," Mrs. Belden said. "I think they are helping my husband lay the fire in the fireplace. After dinner we'll pop some corn, and maybe roast some marshmallows."

"Something smells super!" Jim said as he and Brian

went through the kitchen to get more wood for the living-room fireplace. "What is it?" he asked and sniffed the mixture Trixie was preparing.

"The old Belden stand-by, Moms' hamburgers," Trixie said. "She says you never can make a mistake feeding kids hamburgers."

"Mmmmm, I didn't know anyone could be as hungry as I am," Jim said, as the air filled with the fragrance of baked beans, when Mrs. Belden drew a deep pan from the oven. "Baked beans were my daily fare when I lived in the woods by myself after Ten Acres burned. Mine came cold out of a can, though. There's a subtle difference."

When the food was ready, the Bob-Whites and Mr. and Mrs. Belden sat around the big table in the dining-room, made extra large with two added leaves. At a lower table nearby, the three little boys sat.

At first the twins were shy, but Bobby, loving every minute, soon won them over. "What is hot and cold at the same time?" he asked Terry and Larry. "Don't you tell!" he warned Trixie.

"I don't know," Larry said. "Water?"

"No!" Bobby said. "It's pepper! Jim told me that one."

At the big table the family and guests all joined

hands while Mr. Belden asked the blessing.

Then the fun began.

Dishes were passed from hand to hand, bowls emptied, replenished from the kitchen, emptied again. Mrs. Belden's homemade catsup, old-fashioned beet pickles, corn relish, all disappeared as though by magic, topping the hamburgers. Casseroles of scalloped potatoes, the huge pan of baked beans, all were emptied, salad eaten, and dessert still to come.

Honey, Diana, and Trixie persuaded Mrs. Belden to sit quietly while they carried the plates and other dishes from the table. When the coffee was percolating merrily at Mrs. Belden's right hand, and the cups waiting, hot cocoa or milk in all the children's glasses, the girls brought in generous servings of pumpkin pie.

In the big living-room the fire roared up the chimney, sending a rosy glow over the old shabby room. Chairs and sofas were drawn to face the fireplace, and huge cushions were placed on the floor for the little boys.

The Bob-Whites banished Mr. and Mrs. Belden from the kitchen and attacked the mounds of dishes. They weren't even aware of what they were doing, it was so much fun to do things together.

Trixie, remembering the time that afternoon when Diana and Honey had seemed so impatient with her and had told her she was no fun any more, looked around at their happy faces and was encouraged.

I just wish I needn't ever be so bossy, she thought to herself. *What would I do without Honey and Diana? I guess maybe especially Honey, for she's my very best friend in the whole world.*

Something similar must have been going through Honey's mind because she put her arm around Trixie and hugged her. "I *do* love you so much, Trixie," she whispered, "and everyone in the Belden family."

When they went into the living-room Mr. Belden was playing Simon Says Thumbs Up with Bobby, Terry, and Larry. They were falling all over themselves on the cushions, laughing so hard they couldn't obey one of the "Thumbs Up!" "Thumbs Down!" commands. "You are supposed to obey me *only* when I say 'Simon says,' " Mr. Belden explained. "Try again now, boys."

When the Bob-Whites joined the group around the fireplace, Mr. Belden decided they would add forfeits as a penalty for failing to obey Simon's commands. To make it easier, the forfeits wouldn't apply to the little boys.

"Simon says Thumbs Up!" Mr. Belden said. All the

thumbs went up. "Thumbs Down!" he ordered. Honey and Mart put their thumbs down!

"Simon didn't say it," Mr. Belden explained. "Mart and Honey must pay forfeits. Will you take the forfeits?" he asked Mrs. Belden.

Within half an hour every Bob-White had contributed something, a shoe, a barrette, a wrist watch, a ring, a tie, or a bracelet.

Redeeming the forfeits was lots more fun than the game itself, especially with the forfeits the girls gave.

"I know what to tell Trixie to do," Bobby whispered in his mother's ear.

"Trixie'll never do that, Bobby," his mother said, smiling.

"She'll have to or she won't get her ring back," Bobby insisted. "Go on, Trixie!"

So Trixie stood in the middle of the floor and sang "The Star Spangled Banner." Her voice was true, and she did fairly well until she came to the high notes. "And the rockets red glare . . ." she tried. Her voice cracked and failed, and she dropped to the floor laughing as hard as Bobby.

"Now you tell me what penalty to give Diana," Mrs. Belden said to Terry. The little boy whispered in her ear.

"I'm really going to enjoy this one," Mrs. Belden

said and looked over to where Mart sat on the sofa. Then she whispered the penalty in Diana's ear.

Diana, blushing to the ends of her finger tips, leaned over and brushed Mart's cheek with a kiss.

That was the high point of the forfeits. Everyone was laughing so hard they couldn't go on. Mart, who teased everyone else all the time, had finally had the tables turned on him by the little Lynch twin.

After that they knelt in a circle in the center of the room. Mr. and Mrs. Belden knelt, too.

Trixie started the game.

"I went to New York today," she said.

"What did you buy?" Jim, next to her, asked.

"A fan to fan myself," she said and waved her hand back and forth.

"I went to New York today," Jim then said to Diana on his other side.

"Did you really?" Diana asked. "What did you buy?"

"A rocking chair and a fan," Jim said and rocked back and forth while he fanned.

Down the line it went, each one adding a purchase and acting it out. Most of them wobbled and fell and were out of the game. Terry and Larry and Bobby were tumbling all over themselves trying to rock and fan and do half a dozen other things.

Patch and Reddy ran around the boys barking and adding to the general confusion and fun.

They wouldn't excuse Mr. Belden, at the end of the line, from trying, so he fanned, he rocked, he held an umbrella, he smelled a rose, winked his eyes back of dark glasses, kicked his heels in new shoes, swayed to the music of a record player he bought, and finally fell over trying on a new hat.

Mrs. Belden brought in the popper and corn.

Jim whooped when he saw it. "I couldn't down a grain of corn if my life depended upon it," he said, "after that dinner I ate."

"I could!" Bobby cried.

"I could!" Larry and Terry echoed.

So Mr. Belden brought in the big dishpan lined with waxed paper. Mrs. Belden poured a handful of corn into the popper and handed it to Mr. Belden. It sputtered and crackled and popped in no time into enormous white flakes which Mrs. Belden salted, buttered, and offered to the guests.

"Don't pop another grain!" Honey finally said.

"The twins will burst," Diana insisted, though they shook their heads vigorously. "I never saw them eat so much in all their lives."

"It's the goodest food," Larry said.

"The goodest food in all the world," said Terry, "an' I'm goin' to come here and live with Bobby."

"Oh, Moms, can he? An' Larry, too? Can't they stay forever?"

"I'm afraid not, Bobby, honey," Diana said. "But your mother said you will be able to come and see us soon, and, twinnies, there's Tom now. He's come for all of us."

"I won't go home," Terry sobbed.

"I won't, too," Larry said. "Go home, Tom!"

"Tell me a riddle, Tom," Bobby begged. "Regan always does."

"All right," Tom said, as he helped Diana and Honey button the howling twins into their snow suits. "Listen!" he said and miraculously they listened.

"What did the doughnut say to the layer cake?" Tom asked.

"I don't know," Terry yelled. "Tell me, Tom."

"Don't give up!" Bobby shouted. "Don't tell, Tom!"

"I won't," Tom said, zipping the legs of the twins' suits. "What did it say, Bobby?"

Bobby thought and thought and thought, but he didn't have the answer. "Awright, I give up, too," he finally said. "What did the doughnut say?"

"If I had all your dough I wouldn't be hanging

around this hole," Tom said. "Come on, kids, let's go."

Mrs. Belden brought out some cookies and an extra pumpkin pie and put them in a basket for Tom to take to Celia.

"It's the most fun we've ever had in all our lives," they all insisted as they trooped out. Trixie and the boys followed them, coatless, out to the station wagon.

Bobby called good-by constantly from the doorway, and the twins answered, waving till they almost fell from the seat beside Tom.

Just before they left, Tom called to Trixie, "You've heard about Bull Thompson's Uncle Snipe, haven't you?"

"Yes," said Trixie, wondering. "What about Snipe?"

"He's back at that bookie business on Hawthorne Street, I guess," Tom said. "I saw him the day after Diana's Valentine party driving a big blue and white sedan. Say, he could have been here when the clubhouse was wrecked."

"Blue and white sedan!" Trixie exclaimed. "There was a blue and white sedan stolen that night. I've wondered about that Snipe Thompson . . . he just could have been angry enough at me about Bull to want to burn our clubhouse."

"Sounds like Snipe's doing," Tom said. "I think he's

just out of prison after serving time for robbery. Forget about it tonight, Trixie, but better check on it with Spider in the morning."

"I will. Thanks, Tom. Wait till I tell Spider!"

"That Snipe's a bad one," Tom said. "Well, everyone in?" he asked the Wheelers and the Lynches. "Guess Regan and I are elected to pick up the antiques tomorrow for the show. See you then, Trixie. Let's go, kids."

Chapter 16
The Show Takes Shape

Trixie, Brian, and Mart had set the alarm for seven o'clock. First they had to collect all the mended furniture from the clubhouse and take it to the showroom.

Then the boys had to go to Mrs. Vanderpoel's, to the Wheelers', to half a dozen other places to pick up the antiques to be exhibited. Tom and Regan would be waiting to help.

The Hakaito brothers were due at the showroom at eleven o'clock to arrange their exhibit.

After the antiques were all assembled the Bob-Whites would have to arrange them in the showroom, and in the windows.

Before any of this would be done, however, Trixie had an errand she thought more important than anything else on their schedule.

"Did you hear what Tom said to me just before he left last night?" she asked her mother.

"No. I didn't go out to the car. What was it?"

"I told you that Sergeant Molinson told us the thieves used a blue and white car they stole, to make their getaway from our clubhouse that night, didn't I?"

"Yes, you did, and Mart told me the sergeant told *you* pretty emphatically to stay out of their business," Mrs. Belden said. "I hope you'll take his advice."

"He's a terrible sour-puss," Trixie said. "I can at least call Spider over at Mrs. Vanderpoel's house and tell him. He doesn't go to work till about ten o'clock."

So Trixie called Spider.

When she came back from the telephone her face was serious.

"Spider said he knows Sergeant Molinson won't try to do anything about Snipe Thompson," she said. "At least not till he has more evidence."

"With the antique show tomorrow, why don't you forget about Snipe?" Mart said. "We got the desk back and the swords back. Now forget about it!"

"Mart is right," Mr. Belden said, as he put his coffee cup on the table. "There hasn't been a robbery on Main Street for fifty years—oh, maybe shoplifters in the stores, but that goes on all the time."

"Maybe *this* will worry you, then," Trixie said. "Spider can't be on the job tonight because he has late duty at his intersection. He said he'd go over to the show-room on his own time after eleven o'clock."

"Spider doesn't need to go at all," Mr. Belden said,

"and he knows it. He's only doing it because of his interest in the Bob-Whites. The regular patrolman will be on duty and that's enough protection."

Trixie's face fell. "Doesn't *anyone* feel any responsibility?" she asked.

"I for one am not going to give it another thought," Brian said. "Tom and Regan will be here any minute with the station wagon and pickup truck. I'm going to finish my breakfast and be ready when they come."

"That's an excellent idea," Mr. Belden said.

"Honey and Diana are coming with them," Trixie said. "Tom will go with us to the clubhouse to get a load of things there and then take us to the showroom."

"Here they come now!" Bobby shouted, peering from his place at the table. "Terry and Larry aren't with him. Can I go to their house, Moms? And can we help with the anteeks?"

"Later in the day maybe, Bobby, if the sun comes out and the day is warm. Please try to say 'may I' instead of 'can I,' will you?"

Bobby hid his head. "I don't get to holp with the show at all," he said.

"I know what we'll do this afternoon," Mr. Belden told Bobby. "If it's a warm day I'll go over and get the boys at the Lynches' and we'll all go to Sleepyside and distribute the handbills for the Bob-Whites."

"That will be super!" Trixie said and hugged her little brother. "That will be the biggest 'holp' of all."

There was good hard work to do in the showroom before the girls could even begin to decorate it for the show. The windows were dusty. The floor needed to be cleaned. There was dust everywhere. It would take dozens of pails of water and detergent to make the room presentable. "I don't know *why* we didn't think of this before," Trixie said.

It all looked pretty hopeless till Tom arrived with Celia. "Mrs. Wheeler said I could help you a while," Celia said and she took the mop out of Trixie's hands. "Your mother is sending Mrs. Bruger, your cleaning woman," she told Diana. "We'll soon have the place looking like something. You girls just go ahead and put papers on the shelves and arrange everything."

Honey had brought a roll of flowered shelf edging, and the girls dusted the shelves, tacked the edging in place with thumbtacks, then covered the shelves with fresh white paper.

Along the shelves they arranged a group of duck decoys Tad had brought them. They had belonged to the father of one of the Hawks. When Tad told him about the show, he donated them.

"The ducks look as though they were alive," Trixie said.

"Yes, wasn't it swell of Tad?" Diana asked. "The wooden toys he got for us can go on the next shelf," she went on. "Hand me that old tin peddler's cart, Honey, please. There! Doesn't that look marvelous? Look at all the little tin pans and bowls he has for sale in his cart."

"And the lanterns," Honey said, as she hung a cluster of miniature tin lanterns on the back of the tin peddler's cart. "My little brothers would be thrilled to have a toy like that."

"It would last about ten minutes with Bobby," Trixie said. "Now take this doll-baby buggy, Diana, and put it next on the shelf. Isn't it priceless? The original flowered lining is still in it, and it rolls. See?" Trixie pushed the high, carved wood baby carriage along the shelf to stand back of the peddler's cart.

"They are ours, too, to sell," Trixie added. "They aren't just to exhibit. Tad said the woman gave them to him for us to sell."

"There surely has been a change in Tad," Diana said. "Remember what a goon he used to be?"

"Maybe we just thought so. Maybe *we* were the goons, not Tad," Trixie said.

"That's what Spider seemed to think, didn't he?"

Honey asked. "I like Tad now. I like him very much."

"I guess we all do," Trixie agreed. "Shall we put some of Mrs. Vanderpoel's silver on this other shelf?"

"No," Honey said. "It isn't for sale. Let's try to keep all the things for sale on one side of the room, and the ones for exhibiting on the other side. That way we won't be in danger of selling anything that doesn't belong to us."

Celia and Mrs. Bruger had finished cleaning the main showroom and had moved on behind the partition to put the back room in better order.

Regan and Brian and Mart arrived in the pickup truck and unloaded the first group of antiques for the exhibit side of the room.

The girls just had to leave their work to admire the beautiful old mahogany three-tiered table, the oak Bible box with its lining of blue Williamsburg paper, the pine settle and book rest, and Mrs. Vanderpoel's little old ebony melodeon.

"Do you know what Mrs. Vanderpoel did?" Brian asked as he and Regan settled the melodeon in place. "She let us take that black walnut chest that stands in her living-room. She called it a *kas* or *schrank*. Take a look at it, Trixie. . . . Wait, we'll bring it in next."

Trixie well knew what the big Holland Dutch chest

looked like. She knew, too, that it was Mrs. Vanderpoel's dearest treasure.

On top of the chest the girls arranged the George III silver they had polished the night Bull Thompson had been captured. The old tankards and salvers shone against the waxed walnut background.

Tom arrived then with a second load of furniture from the clubhouse. Mr. Maypenny, drawn into service, had helped him load them. Now the boys, Brian, Jim, and Mart, arrayed them on the sale side of the room. There were the cherry gate-leg tables that were Mart's pride, the wooden Indian from the Wheelers' attic, the gilt mirror, which stood on its base, the Pembroke table, some ladder-back chairs that came from Mrs. Vanderpoel's lean-to kitchen, several odds and ends of wall whatnots, and some painted chairs.

"Mrs. Wheeler told me to take this, and not to put it in anyone's hands but yours," Tom said. He handed the doll trunk to Trixie.

"It's the gold musical jewel box!" Trixie cried, delighted. "I haven't seen it for weeks. Isn't it the most beautiful thing you ever saw?" Carefully Trixie took it from the small doll trunk and set it, for exhibit, on top of the Chippendale three-tiered table, just inside the front window.

"It almost knocks your eyes out, doesn't it?" Mart asked.

"Yes, and we'd never have had it either," Diana said, "if Trixie hadn't snooped till she found it hidden in the chimney."

"I don't like the word 'snooped,' " Trixie said indignantly. "Oh, here are the Hakaito brothers with their swords and things. Isn't this the most fun in the whole world? Jeepers, I told them I'd have some Japanese lanterns hung in the corner where they are going to put their Japanese display. Here's the ladder. Help me, will you please, Jim?"

Jim brought the ladder to the corner just as the Hakaito brothers came in smiling, their arms full of carefully wrapped tissue bundles.

"*We* hang lanterns," Oto said. "Later, when exhibit is in place. Now we work. You see later." He adjusted a tall Japanese screen to close off the corner.

Jim turned around, held out his hands palms up, and shrugged. "That's that!" he said.

While they had been talking, Diana and Honey had been busy. In the corner opposite the one where the Japanese brothers were working, on the sales side, they hung two lengths of clothesline. To these they pinned the aprons they had made. The gay-flowered patterns and bright colors made a lovely picture.

Back of the aprons, and above them, so they were in plain view, the stuffed elephants, kittens, dogs, tigers, and bears ranged in patterned calico. Beside them the dolls sat primly, their kapok-stuffed toes hanging over the edge of the shelf.

"We'll have to put the price tags on these later," Honey said. "Here they are." She took a handful of white paper squares from her pocket and put them on the shelf. "It won't take long."

"I'm getting so excited," Trixie said as she stood off to look at the other girls' work. "The room looks simply gorgeous!"

"It does!" Mr. Belden said as he stepped through the door, followed by three sturdy little boys, their hands full of sale bills. "I never guessed you had done so much work on this show." Mr. Belden put his arm proudly around Trixie's shoulders.

"I kept trying to tell you what it would be like, Daddy," Trixie said, her eyes shining. "Did you have fun?" she asked the little boys who stood with big eyes in front of the toy shelves staring at the array of colorful animals.

"Yes, we did, Trixie," Bobby said. "We put the bills in people's letter boxes, didn't we, Daddy?"

"They did," Mr. Belden said. "They worked like little beavers."

"We worked so hard we're tired," Larry and Terry said. "We want to eat."

Trixie sighed. "I guess we all want to eat," she said. "What time is it, Daddy?"

"Almost twelve o'clock," her father answered. "If we hurry over to Wimpy's, we can get in before the crowd comes."

"We'll *be* the crowd," Mart said. "I'm starved. We'll fill all the seats at Wimpy's."

"Wait till we wash our hands," Trixie called. "Come on, Celia, Tom, Regan, Mrs. Bruger, Bob-Whites. How about you?" she called around the screen to the Hakaito brothers.

"We stay here," they announced. "We finish work first."

"I'll stay, too," Celia said. "I wouldn't go anyplace in this old work uniform!"

"I'll stay, too, with Celia," Tom said. "Bring something back for us, Trixie."

Mrs. Bruger, the cleaning woman, refused to go, too, so the rest of them trooped out.

Trixie was glad the showroom wouldn't be deserted. There were so many valuable antiques there.

"I haven't seen a sign of one of Sergeant Molinson's men all day," she said.

"What would a policeman be doing around today?" Mart asked. "With all of us there? The sergeant," he added airily to his father, "seems unaccountably unable to appreciate the quality of my beloved sibling's flat-footing."

"Whoops! There goes my appetite!" Trixie shouted. "Ask him to define the words, Daddy. I know he doesn't know what they mean. What are you going to order, Bobby?"

"Hamburger!" Bobby shouted. "Me and Larry and Terry want hamburgers."

"The same thing all around," Mr. Belden said. "Right, kids?"

Terry and Larry created a scene when their orders came. "Take mine back!" Terry shouted. "It's no good. I want one like I had last night."

"Me, too," Larry echoed.

"Who made 'em?" Mike, the counter man, asked, bewildered.

"My moms!" Bobby cried, laughing and beating on the counter. "An' hers are the goodest," he said, filling his mouth.

"Maybe we could get her to work here," Mike said

sarcastically. "Take 'em or leave 'em, kids. People are lined up back of you waitin' for 'em."

"It takes the kids to tell them, doesn't it?" Jim asked on the way back to the showroom. "We aren't going to be very popular with Mike for a while."

"It's all in a day's work to him," Brian said.

"*Our* day's work is far from done," Trixie said. "I'll walk over to the car with Daddy and the boys if you'll take the food back to Tom and Celia and Mrs. Bruger. They must be starved."

"I ordered some extra for the Hakaito brothers," her father said. "Come on, boys!" He and Trixie herded the little boys ahead of them into the car.

"Oh, by the way," her father said. "I forgot and left this copy of *The Sleepyside Sun* in the car. I was going to give it to you. There's a half-page spread about the show."

"An' pictures of the jewel box," Bobby added, "an' Mrs. Vanderpoel's silver, an'—"

"All right, Bobby, let's go," his father said. "Trixie will see it for herself."

Chapter 17
Brom's Surprise

When Trixie went back to the showroom she found that the Hakaito brothers had finished their part of the exhibit. A thin bamboo curtain hung in front of the corner, closing it off from the rest of the room.

"Please to see exhibit of swords, Miss Trixie," Oto said and drew aside the curtain.

Back of the curtain there was a land of enchantment. The two walls were hung with scrolls of vivid, painted Japanese warriors, in various phases of their swordplay.

"These are swords that warriors use in Japanese drama," Oto explained, indicating the swords and daggers surrounding the scrolls.

On shelves on one wall the Japanese brothers had displayed little silk-clad dolls depicting the famous cherry blossom dance in Tokyo, little painted ladies in gaily flowered kimonos and carrying tiny, delicate fans.

Trixie was fascinated. She put her hand up, to set in motion a series of tinkling glass wind bells which hung from the shelves. The other Bob-Whites gathered around back of her, eyes big with wonder.

On the opposite wall, on shelves, exquisite ivories were arranged, little rickshas pulled by miniature Japanese men, boxes which when opened revealed other boxes, and inside them still other boxes, all carved in lacy patterns. There were small birds and lotus flowers, little ivory sampans and lovely ladies, bearded old men and Japanese gods. From the shelves, to match the wind bells on the opposite wall, hung delicate black enameled cricket cages skillfully woven of reeds.

"You like it, Miss Trixie?" Oto asked.

The Bob-Whites burst into spontaneous clapping.

"It's marvelous!" Trixie said. "We should charge extra just to let people see it. It's the loveliest, most beautiful, most—"

"Artistic, charming, exquisite, superb, magnificent . . ." Mart supplied, and Trixie nodded vigorously.

"For once in your life, Mart," she said, "you've run out of words. How can we ever repay you for doing this?" she asked the Hakaito brothers.

"We repaid already," Oto said, and Kasyo added, his grin widening to his ears, "Miss Honey tell her cook Hakaito brothers have best vegetables."

"And very good fruits," Oto added. "We go now."

"Just think," Trixie said. "If we hadn't been going to have our show we'd never have known Oto and Kasyo."

"Yes," Jim agreed, "and here we are thinking we're doing so much for people all over the world, and these two Japanese men take time out from their work—and they work terribly hard—to do this for us."

"Not so much for us," Diana reminded him, "as for the United Nations Children's Fund. I *do* hope we make a lot of money."

"We'd better get busy and finish this room, if we're ever going to be through in time to open tomorrow," Brian said. "Look at that, there's Spider! I thought you said he was on duty and couldn't watch our exhibit for us."

"He's off duty this afternoon," Trixie said, "and *on* duty till eleven o'clock tonight. After that, he said he'd watch things."

"Will you look who's with him?" Mart said. "Mrs. Vanderpoel!"

"And—it can't be—it *is* Brom!" Trixie said.

The little Dutch woman came bustling in, her hat askew over her blue eyes and pink cheeks. "I'd have had to stay home if it hadn't been for Spider," she said, "and I did want to come in today. I don't want to be here tomorrow with everyone gallivantin' around. I want to see what you have, without a lot of people around who don't know a trivet from a warming pan."

"It's grand to have you here," Trixie said, "and you, too, Mr. Brom," she said to the old man who hovered close to Spider's side. "Bobby just left about half an hour ago. His heart will be broken because he didn't see you."

"We're going to stop at Crabapple Farm on the way home so Brom can see Bobby," Spider said. "That was part of the bait I used to get Brom to come with us."

Mart took the old gentleman in charge and walked around the showroom with him, explaining just who owned the various articles exhibited. Brom knew the old families and their history back to colonial days. He grew more talkative as Trixie joined them, and he told bits of history of early New York.

When they came to the carved lap desk he paused, seemed a little confused.

"That's the desk those crooks stole from Bobby and me that day we were at Mrs. Vanderpoel's house," Trixie said.

The little old Dutch woman, hearing her name, crossed the room.

"I was showing Mr. Brom the desk," Trixie said. "We'd surely like to know who it was that brought it to the old schoolhouse the night of the blizzard."

Brom's face turned dull red. He fidgeted and tried to turn away.

"It's no secret," Mrs. Vanderpoel said. "Brom did it."

"Jumpin' Jeepers Jehoshaphat," Mart said, drawing in his breath. "He did? How?"

"I tracked that boy down," Brom said, "that no-good boy who was shovelin' the walks that day and ran away without his pay."

"Brom was sure he had something to do with stealing that desk," Mrs. Vanderpoel explained. "So he shadowed the poolrooms in town till he saw the boy."

"Then I followed him to where he lived," Brom said and added triumphantly, "and there was that desk. I saw it through the window of his house, settin' right there on a table as big as life!"

Jim and Honey and Brian joined the group, hearing bits of the conversation.

"How on earth did you ever get it out of his house?" Jim asked.

"Stole it back!" the old man said, laughing and slapping his sides. "He didn't know what hit him! I just opened the door, went up back of him, buckled his knees, knocked him down, took the desk, and high-tailed out of there!"

"He just told me about it a short time ago," Mrs. Vanderpoel said. "He's smart as a fox, Brom is, isn't he?" she asked Trixie.

"Yes . . . yes, he is," Trixie agreed enthusiastically, then looked at Jim, her forehead wrinkled in puzzlement.

"That doesn't tell the whole story," she said. "How did it ever get outside that schoolhouse the night of the blizzard? That's still a problem for the Belden-Wheeler Detective Agency to try and solve."

"Wasn't no problem at all," Brom said. "*I* did it."

"You went out in that blizzard to leave that desk at the schoolhouse?" Trixie asked. "That's pretty hard to believe."

"Believe it or not," the old man said with spirit, "I've been trampin' those woods for seventy years, winter and summer, and I know 'em better than a fox or a rabbit."

"That may even be so," Jim said, scratching his head, "but why on earth didn't you just give it back to us at the clubhouse, or at Mrs. Vanderpoel's house, or Crabapple Farm?"

"Because I live not five hundred feet from the old schoolhouse," Brom said.

"You just stop askin' any more questions, all of you; you got your desk back, didn't you?" Mrs. Vanderpoel said. "Getting an old man all stirred up just because he set that trap that Reddy got caught in, and wanted to make it up to Bobby! Bunch of busybodies!" the old woman said scornfully.

"Now, now," Brom said, "let's be friends. I shouldn't have set that trap, and you know it. Just tryin' to earn a little money gatherin' fox pelts. I should have thought of a dog gettin' caught. Desk looks mighty pretty settin' there," Brom said, "and all the rest of Mrs. Vanderpoel's things. Ain't none of them, even the foreign things, any prettier. Would you like to put this on top of the desk, Trixie?"

Brom fumbled in the big pocket of his overcoat and brought out a child's antique bank. An iron man sat in an iron chair with his iron hand held out in front of him, palm up. Brom dropped a penny in the outstretched hand. The iron man nodded his thanks, reached around with his iron hand, and dropped the penny in a money slot.

"It's marvelous!" Trixie cried. "It's darling, and so are you!" she said and gave the old gentleman a hug.

His face grew red but he smiled from ear to ear and patted Trixie's arm.

"Sell the bank," he said. "It's for all those little kids who're hungry."

When Spider had taken Mrs. Vanderpoel and Brom away, a sober-faced group of young people went back to their work.

"If we *never* hear another word of thanks for what we've done," Trixie said, "I'd do all the work over again a dozen times just to get to know people like Brom and Mrs. Vanderpoel, and Oto and Kasyo."

"You said it!" Mart agreed. "And Spider and Tad, too."

"And that goes for Tom and Regan and Celia and Mrs. Bruger, and Mr. Maypenny and everyone else who has helped us . . . all the people who let us take their antiques . . . and our parents . . ." Trixie said.

"Sleepyside is a wonderful place. I'm glad I live here," Honey said.

"Yeah," Mart said. "Who'd want to live any other place on earth?"

Chapter 18
Night Watch

"Oh, Moms, it's the most beautiful place!" Trixie, starry-eyed, sat at the table and unfolded her napkin. "Why didn't you come to see the showroom? Even Mrs. Vanderpoel and Brom came in. It looks like fairyland."

"Daddy hasn't talked of anything else, and neither has Bobby, ever since they came home. I'm so proud of all of you. I thought I'd go tomorrow, and tonight I'd have a good warm dinner waiting," Mrs. Belden said. "Eat something, dear."

"I just don't seem to have any appetite," Trixie said dreamily. "You should see the way that musical jewel box looks, Moms. And the Japanese exhibit, and Mrs. Vanderpoel's silver . . ."

"I know it's wonderful, dear, but do eat your dinner now and forget about the show until tomorrow."

"I *have* to talk about it, Moms," Trixie said. "Daddy, why do you suppose the policeman on that beat didn't stop in to see us? We waited a long time thinking he would pass the showroom."

"Gosh, Trixie, are you going to start that all over

again?" Mart asked. "Dad, she hasn't talked about any-thing else. If she had her way, she'd sit up all night and watch."

"I would not, Mart Belden," Trixie declared. "Did you happen to notice how that musical jewel box shows up through the window? It's an invitation to thieves."

"Of course I noticed it. You can't seem to get it through your head that right across the street, in the bank, there are thousands and thousands of dollars. You don't see Dad going into a nose dive over it every night, do you?" Mart was tired and cross.

"He doesn't have moneybags in the window for all the thieves to see," Trixie said, "and he has vaults and things with big time locks. And besides, he hasn't had anyone named Snipe Thompson waiting to grab the moneybags. Two of those thieves are still at large, and we know right well one of them is that horrible Snipe."

"That's enough, Trixie," Mr. Belden said. "I wish you would please stop talking about it. Everything will be safe. Just stop worrying, will you please?"

"Yes, Daddy," Trixie said obediently and she tried to eat her dinner.

She didn't stop worrying, though. After she went to bed she couldn't go to sleep. *After all,* she thought to her-self, *Daddy didn't* see *those thieves who hijacked the desk. He didn't* see *Bull Thompson when he broke into Mrs. Vanderpoel's house. He didn't* see *the way that clubhouse looked when those robbers tried to set it on fire. He didn't* see *Snipe Thompson . . . well, neither did I but he's a bad man.*

Trixie turned and tossed, one name going through her mind time and time again . . . Snipe Thompson. "Why didn't I *insist* that Sergeant Molinson bring Snipe in and question him?" she asked herself. "Why didn't I? Because the sergeant wouldn't have done it. He didn't pay any attention to me when I tried to get him to investigate that blue and white sedan. How do I know he even inquired at the pawnbroker's? How do I know he'll pay any attention to the showroom now? But Daddy said . . ."

The clock ticked on. Trixie just couldn't sleep. The house was quiet. Trixie's mind was not quiet.

Finally she could stand it no longer. She turned on the light. Her desk clock said eleven o'clock. It was time Spider was showing up at the showroom *if* he had any intention of watching it.

Quietly Trixie put on her clothes, opened her door, listened, heard nothing, then tiptoed down the stairs. She reached for her coat in the hall closet, and a scarf, then went outside and down the walk to the road that led to Sleepyside.

She hadn't gone far when, back of her, she heard the unmistakable chug of Brian's car. He pulled up opposite her and stopped. "Have you lost your mind?" he asked. "It's after eleven."

"I know it. You can go right back home," Trixie said. "You aren't going to stop me."

"Who said I was? I'm wide-awake now and might as well go in and give the place the once-over. Say, Trixie, isn't that Jim up ahead?"

It was. Laughing, he climbed into Brian's jalopy. "We all had the same idea, didn't we?"

"Yes," Trixie said, "and I thought I was the only one who worried. Gleeps, I'm glad you're both going. Moms and Dad won't be quite so mad at *me*. How did you happen to get your jalopy out without anyone hearing it, Brian?"

"I left it down the road, opposite the driveway. Didn't you notice it?"

"I did not. And that means you intended to go into town all the time. Did you, too, Jim?" Trixie asked.

Jim didn't answer.

"I like that!" Trixie said. "You weren't going to say a thing to me about it, and you pretended I woke you, Brian."

"We thought you'd been in enough danger," Jim tried to explain.

"Thank you very much for your concern, Jim Frayne," Trixie said. "Oh, all right. I'm here. We don't have time to argue. I just hope Moms and Daddy don't wake up and find we're gone."

"That's a chance I had to take with my family," Jim said. "Brian, turn down the street next to Main Street, then come back and park east of the showroom. Maybe we'll run into Spider."

A lone light shone faintly in the showroom, back in the corner opposite the Japanese exhibit.

Spider came to meet them from the drugstore nearby. "I *thought* some of the Bob-Whites would be showing up," he said. "I have the key to the building right next to the showroom. A man I know who has an office upstairs said I could use his office. We can go up there and keep watch through the window."

"Did you see the regular patrolman anyplace around?" Trixie asked.

"He only passes here about every hour," Spider answered. "He spends most of his time patrolling the alleys that lead off of Main Street to Hawthorne Street. That's one reason I wanted to come down and keep an eye on things myself tonight. I don't think anything will happen, but I know you kids are worried about those borrowed antiques."

Trixie, Brian, and Jim followed Spider to the window in the second-story office. The street down below was almost deserted. Now and then a car went by, but the pedestrians were few.

There was an excellent view of the front of the showroom building. No one could possibly enter without being seen by the four watchers stationed opposite.

Trixie never left the window. Brian and Jim and Spider were not quite so vigilant. Now that they were within sight of the showroom they seemed to feel more secure. They sat around a desk in the office talking.

The minute hand on the clock began its slow journey around the dial. It was eleven fifteen. Then eleven thirty.

Brian and Jim, restless, walked around the room, unable to keep still. Trixie shuffled her feet in the chair where she sat watching.

"Why don't you kids go on home?" Spider asked. "You need sleep if you're going to be on the job all day tomorrow. Don't you see how quiet everything is? I'll stay around here till it starts to get daylight."

"We'll stay a while longer," Jim insisted. "We haven't been here an hour."

"Yes," Brian said, "we'll get plenty of sleep, because the show doesn't open till nine o'clock in the morning."

"We'll get the heebie-jeebies just standing around," Spider said. "Anyone want to play cards?" He drew a pack of cards from his pocket. "How about it, Trixie?"

"I was thinking that if you'll give me the key," Trixie said, "I'll go down to the showroom and finish putting the price tags on the dolls and aprons. It's the only thing we didn't finish."

"Better not," Spider said. "If you turn up the lights, someone passing is sure to think something's wrong."

"I don't need to turn the light up. I can work under that bulb in the corner," Trixie insisted. "It won't take me long. Then I guess we'd better go on home, maybe, if Spider is going to stay here anyway."

"Want me to go along, Trixie?" Jim asked.

"I'll be okay, Jim," Trixie answered. "You stay and play cards with Spider and Brian. This job will only take a few minutes."

Trixie let herself into the showroom. *Everything's so beautiful,* she thought. *And it's so quiet.*

She found the square paper slips where Honey had left them on the shelf beside the lines of aprons. Carefully she spread the slips under the light and went to work.

A car went noisily by outside. It disappeared in the distance, but another sound took its place—a faint shuffle, a shuffle that came from—the back room!

Startled, Trixie put down the paper tag she was working on, and listened.

"Keep right on at what you were doing, sister!" a hoarse voice whispered.

Trixie jumped to her feet.

"An' sit down!" the voice ordered. "Don't make a move! Think you're pretty smart, don't you, sendin' my nephew to reform school? Now it's your turn for trouble! Sit down!"

Snipe Thompson! Trixie, shaking from head to toe, obeyed, sat back in the chair.

"Now you bend over that desk like you was workin'," Snipe ordered. "I know your brother and that Wheeler kid and that fly cop Webster are upstairs next door. I want 'em to stay there just a little bit longer. You bein' here makes it easier for us. We'll promise you a little ride when we get through, sister, to pay you for your kindness. Get busy at what you were doin'!"

Trixie, frantic, not knowing which way to turn, did as Snipe ordered and tried to write the tags.

Automatically the Bob-White distress call formed on her lips. *They'll kill me for sure if I make any kind of a noise,* she thought. *What can I do?*

Her fingers clenched the pencil. Almost without

thinking about it, she began to draw three little stick figures on the tags:

Mechanically she continued drawing the same figures, her heart pounding so she could scarcely breathe.

"Bring that gold box back here!" Snipe commanded hoarsely. "Just pick it up and walk right back here. Get some of that silver on your way."

At Snipe's command Trixie went back and forth, back and forth, till all the silver had been carried out and seized by two masked figures.

As Trixie turned to go back into the showroom after every last bit of silver had been carried out, she saw Jim leave the entrance to the building next door. "Thank goodness," she breathed and stood still in the partition doorway to try to obscure Snipe's view.

It was too late!

"Get back in there and keep workin' on those tags!" Snipe commanded. "Don't say a word about us! I'll have a gun trained on you every second. If that guy mentions the silver, tell him you took it out back for safekeeping. If you spill one word I'll drill both of you!"

Jim turned the knob and came into the showroom.

"It seemed to be taking you a long time so I thought I'd see what had happened, Trixie," he said. "Is everything all right?"

"Yes, Jim," Trixie answered slowly. "Everything's all right. I'm just tagging the aprons, see?"

Then an idea flashed through her mind. "Take a look at the tags," she said. "See if you think the prices are right." Trixie gathered up a few of the paper squares topped with her SOS call.

"I'll put them here on the desk and go on pinning others on the aprons," she said, mindful of Snipe's warning not to approach Jim. "Maybe you'll think the prices are too high. Go over to the desk and look at them, Jim."

"How do I know anything about the price of aprons?" Jim asked. "Whatever you and Honey have decided is all right. Will it take you much longer to finish your work?"

"I don't think so, Jim." Trixie's voice was tense. "I'd feel better if you'd *please* check on the prices we're asking," Trixie begged, near despair.

Jim only waved his hand to show he wasn't interested. "Whatever you and the other girls have decided," he said, "goes for me."

"We got some of the prices out of that page in the *St. Nicholas,*" Trixie said desperately. "That page of figures in that old magazine we found in the attic."

"I don't know what you're talking about, Trixie. Get the job finished as soon as you can. We'll wait about another fifteen or twenty minutes and then I think we'd better be moving on home. Nothing around here to worry about. Say, Trixie, wasn't there a lot of silver out here on display? That was what worried you, wasn't it? You thought it showed too much from the street. Did you put it under cover?"

The chest where the silver had stood was next to the desk where Trixie had been filling out the tags. Jim walked over to it as he finished his question. "Hid it someplace, did you?" he asked.

Trixie, conscious of Snipe's gun, forced herself to answer casually, "Yes, Jim. I put it out of sight."

"Good girl!" Jim applauded. "Soon as you're through we'll go home. I'll go get Brian. We'll be back in a jiff."

When Jim stood at the chest inquiring about the silver, Trixie made a last frightened effort to communicate with him. If *only* he had looked at her she could have formed words with her lips. He didn't. In a flash, though, frantically, she dropped into Jim's coat pocket a handful of the paper squares she had been marking. At the top of each one was the Bob-White coded call for help:

It was almost a hopeless gesture. Jim would never find the SOS call in time. How *could* he?

Utterly helpless, Trixie watched Jim walk across the room, open the door, and leave.

"Good thing for you you didn't squeal!" the coarse voice from the back room whispered. "You're a smart cooky. Now bring back that carved desk the whiskered old gent stole from us an' . . . what'd you say?" he asked the man with him. "Oh, yeah, the swords, too. My frien' here says it's a matter of honor to get 'em both back, desk an' swords."

Painfully and slowly, for she was almost fainting with fear, Trixie picked up the carved lap desk and carried it to the back room. It was her first glimpse of Snipe. One look at his vicious unshaven face filled her with new terror. He grabbed the desk from her roughly, then commanded, "Go back and get the swords we had—an' a couple more for good measure!"

Two lumpy dirty bags filled with silver and the

jewel box were piled at the back door. The door was at the far end of the back room. *We couldn't see that door from upstairs,* Trixie thought sadly. *Jim and Brian and Spider can't see it now. Everything we have is going to be stolen and I'll—*

"Get goin', sister!" Snipe ordered. "The swords!"

Jim will never find those paper squares, never *in all the world . . . they'll just find my body somewhere . . . oh, Moms! Daddy!*

Hopelessly Trixie took the samurai swords from the wall. Slowly she went toward the back room. Snipe stood inside the door, his greedy hands stretched out. "Now come with us, sister," he said. "We like your company."

"Reach for the sky!" a sharp voice commanded from the alley door.

Spider stood there, his revolver covering Snipe and his accomplice.

"Drop your gun!" he ordered Snipe's pal who held the sawed-off shotgun aimed at Trixie.

"Frisk 'em both!" Spider said to Jim and Brian.

Trixie, in the door, dropped the samurai swords and, with an exultant cry, picked up the dropped shotgun and thrust it in Jim's hands. "Shoot 'em in the legs!" she shouted hysterically. "Then they'll never get away!

Oh, Spider! Oh, Jim! Oh, Brian!" Her knees buckled and she dropped into a nearby chair.

Jim and Brian quickly tied the arms of the two men. Spider's shrill whistle brought the patrolman on the run. He summoned the patrol car, and, when it came, the trussed thieves were loaded into it.

Where scarcely a soul had been on the street a few moments before, a crowd milled. Brian and Jim, and Trixie, too, who had recovered miraculously, restored the nearly stolen articles to their places in the showroom.

Then they watched while Spider nailed bars across the back door.

With a quick look around, the trio went out the front door, locked it behind them, and crossed the street to Brian's jalopy.

"I never want to live through another half hour like that one," Trixie said wearily. "Why *couldn't* you see that I was trying to tell you something, Jim?"

"I'm just dumb, I guess, Trixie," Jim said unhappily. "I thought you'd really flipped when you kept talking about the price of the aprons."

"But I tried so hard to let you know. Snipe held that gun on me all the time."

"Let's not think of that," Brian said, clutching the wheel of his jalopy tightly.

"I even tried to tell you about that page in *St. Nicholas* magazine," Trixie went on.

"I know," Jim said. "That's what made me wonder when I went back upstairs. It sounded so crazy."

"How *did* you finally find out?" Trixie asked. "Did you find the SOS?"

"*Did* he?" Brian shouted. "He pulled that bunch of price tags out of his pocket when he stuffed his gloves in there. He hit the ceiling!"

"Then we all hit the stairs!" Jim added. "I'd like to get my hands on that Snipe Thompson!"

"He'll go to prison now for sure," Trixie said. "Maybe he'll stay there this time. Gee, I hope Moms and Dad won't be mad at me."

"They won't be," Brian said. "They're pretty swell!"

The next day crowds thronged the showroom from the opening hour until it closed. Every article on the sales side of the room was sold, with orders for more.

Mr. Stratton and the members of the school board all came. They bought things and walked around as proudly as though they had originated the idea of the antique show.

At eight o'clock Jim and Trixie locked the front door and drew the blinds. All the borrowed antiques had to be returned to the owners that night. Regan and Tom carried them to the waiting station wagon and pickup truck parked in back of the building.

"Forget them," Regan told the Bob-Whites. "Tom and I'll deliver them."

Spider put the day's receipts into a strongbox and handed the heavy box to Trixie for safekeeping.

At home in the Belden kitchen, Trixie, Honey, Diana, Jim, Brian, and Mart counted the money.

The total sent them whooping around the kitchen like Indians.

It amounted to $763.94!

"We still haven't sold the rings that were in the musical jewel box," Jim said. "I don't know how much more money that will mean."

"Spider's almost sure Trixie will get a reward for helping capture Snipe Thompson and his pal," Mart said. "Do you know, I think the detective business may not be a bad business to get into after all. This is about the third reward Trixie will have had."

"If there *is* any reward, it will go into the UNICEF fund," Trixie said, "and," she added ruefully, "Moms said there must be no more detective work till school's out."

"Did you promise?" Honey asked hopefully.

"No," Trixie said, her blue eyes brightening. "No, I don't believe Moms asked me to promise."

Trixie Belden is back!

Don't miss any of her exciting adventures.

Trixie Belden #1
The Secret of the Mansion

Trixie Belden #2
The Red Trailer Mystery

Trixie Belden #3
The Gatehouse Mystery

Trixie Belden #4
The Mysterious Visitor

Trixie Belden #5
The Mystery off Glen Road

Trixie Belden #6
The Mystery in Arizona

Trixie Belden #7
The Mysterious Code

Trixie Belden #8
The Black Jacket Mystery

Trixie Belden #9
The Happy Valley Mystery